As Julian complimented Rosalind, a little shine of excitement came to her eyes and a flush to her cheeks.

Then she suddenly grew cold, her face set in haughty lines, a remote expression coming into her eyes. For she had just remembered that she was not supposed to be smiling up into his face. Rosalind's plan had been to arouse his interest, then to snub him, to bewilder him with such contempt that when Harriet—with her sweetness and sympathy—next came into his view, she would seem just the thing to mend his bruised sensibilities.

Just as suddenly, however, Rosalind changed again. She was using the wrong tactics. She forced her face into a provocative smile, set her eyelids blinking, and tossed her head flirtatiously.

Julian was by now totally bewildered with this enchanting young lady.' . . .

A
Regency
Rose

Miriam Lynch

FAWCETT COVENTRY • NEW YORK

A REGENCY ROSE

Published by Fawcett Coventry Books, a unit of CBS Publications, the Consumer Publishing Division of CBS Inc.

Copyright © 1980 by Miriam Lynch

ISBN: 0-449-50031-4

Printed in the United States of America

First Fawcett Coventry Printing: March 1980

10   9   8   7   6   5   4   3   2   1

1

It was a dull day, and some of the gloom of the weather seemed to have seeped into Lady Bannestock's sewing chamber, for three of the women in it, variously occupied, were plainly not in a talkative mood.

Only Lady Mary herself, who had little sensibility, chattered on, unaware that she was not being attentively listened to. Sir Charles Bannestock, her good-natured husband, described her as a "prattle-box" but actually enjoyed the prosing, some of which often grew so tangled and muddled that it made little sense, for it did not call from him any effort to reply and left his mind clear for other concerns.

Standing upon a low footstool, now and then squirming with impatience, Miss Rosalind Bannestock suffered the boredom of having Lady Mary's old ball gown fitted to her figure. There knelt at her feet Jane Biggers, her ladyship's dresser, who wore an affronted expression that seemed to draw her long, thin face down even further. Her feelings, easily bruised, were sadly out of temper at being forced to serve in such a manner this lowly member of the household.

It was hopeless to try to make a silk purse out of a sow's ear, she told herself scornfully. The girl might have a perfect figure for the fashion in gowns this year (the high waist and the softly falling skirt trimmed with wide ruffles at the hem) but she was a country girl; and Biggers, who had served her ladyship since that worthy woman's marriage to Sir Charles, had the contempt of London servants for anyone born and raised in the hinterlands.

And, in Biggers opinion, Rosalind's sister was even more hopelessly out of the *ton*. Miss Harriet Bannestock sat in a far corner of the room with a pile of mending on her lap. Which only went to show her lack of standing in the household, Biggers sniffed to herself. She might consider herself a member of the family, but that was only by an accident of birth, and the fact that they were here in this luxurious house in Grosvenor Square—along with their odious young brother—was not at all from her ladyship's choice but because of her Christian sense of duty. Confirming this thought for Biggers was Lady Mary's wandering monologue which at last caught the attention of all three.

". . . Do very well for your come-out ball, Rosalind. Quite impossible to buy you a complete new wardrobe," and she sighed so deeply that her ample bosom quivered. "Too bad you cannot wear those things from which Harriet got so little use last year. But they should be recognized, I fear, and I should be put down as clutch-fisted. I can just hear the tittle-tattle there would be at Almack's should you appear in your sister's old clothes."

"But *this!*"

Rosalind looked down at the stiff material, creamy white and figured with tiny roses almost lost in the dull design, which was not at all in the mode.

Even she, indifferent as she was to fashion, was aware of that. Although Biggers might manage to perform a miracle and make the gown fit, it would still look like what it was—a made-over garment which had once belonged to someone not at all of her height and figure.

She was a tall girl, although not as tall as Miss Harriet, who was so conscious of her height that she often had to be scolded for walking with her head dropped forward. Thus her fine, gray green eyes were not easily seen by those who dismissed her as a "Long Peg" and did not appreciate the flawless, healthy complexion of one who had spent many hours out of doors.

Rosalind was the prettier of the two. She had a pert little nose, brilliantly blue eyes and rich, chestnut hair which curled easily and softly. While not the great beauty her cousin, Corinna Bannestock, was, she was an uncommonly bonny girl; and Lady Mary was willing to concede that, but Rosalind's round little face with its ripe-apple cheeks trembled as Lady Mary enlarged upon the subject which Rosalind had hoped fervently would not arise again this day.

"Speaking of your come-out, my dear, there are things you must remember. It is not enough for a girl to have pretty manners and be pleasing to the eye. Every year there are a dozen of that kind fired off. You must make yourself agreeable to the gentlemen by treating them with admiration, as though they were the last word in wisdom and intelligence. Let us hope that this year there will not be another failure."

Rosalind cast a quick glance at her sister. Although Harriet's head was bent over the shirt she was mending, there was enough of her face in view to display the painful flush upon it.

It was not necessary for anything more to be said. The thoughts of all four in the sewing chamber were the same: Harriet, who had come out the season before, had not attracted a single suitor. Not only had no one offered for her, there had not been the usual morning calls by the gentlemen she had met during the rounds of routs and balls and Venetian breakfasts; not a single trinket or posy had been delivered; even the fireplace mantel in the bedroom she shared with Rosalind had grown devoid of invitation cards by the end of the first month of her season.

Harriet had suffered that most dreaded of fates for a

young woman on the marriage market—she had not "taken," a circumstance her uncle's wife had not let her forget for an instant.

Of the two sisters, it was Rosalind who felt the failure more severely. Younger by a year, she still had been fiercely protective of the other girl, suffering when Harriet was hurt—dear, quiet, serious-minded Harriet; if men did not appreciate her qualities, then it was indeed their loss. This she muttered under her breath so that no one heard her except Biggers, who lifted her head and threw her a look of deep dislike. At that moment, Rosalind would have willingly surrendered her own chances of making a successful come-out (if, indeed, she might do so) in Lady Mary's made-over gown.

"What are you saying?" her ladyship demanded. "You must not mumble. It is not becoming!" She heaved another monstrous sigh, and her face drooped in a martyred expression. "It does not seem, no matter how hard I try, that there is any gratitude on the part of you two girls. I have done my best, I vow. When Sir Charles insisted that you come here to live, your parents having died and no one else to care for you, I made no objection. Haven't I given you and your brother everything needed to make you all happy? Did I not try my best with you, Harriet?"

The girl's head dropped further forward and her drooping shoulders bespoke her misery. Lady Mary went on in the same complaining voice. "I must admit that I was sorely disappointed when no man fixed his interest upon you. You will soon be twenty, and then it will be too late. As for you, Rosalind, you seem not to appreciate your chance. Since neither of you has any competence—your father having left you nothing except that encumbered estate in Sussex—it will be most difficult to make a favorable connection for you. Now what is it that you're saying? I have asked you not to mumble."

Rosalind, with a toss of her head, returned, "I said, Aunt Mary, that it is very much like a livestock sale. Do they not call Almack's the 'marriage mart'? Don't young ladies go on view exactly like cows brought to market?"

There was a chorus of gasps from the throats of the other three women. They were plainly appalled by the uttering of such heresy. Even Harriet, who might secretly believe in the truth of her sister's assertion, stared round-eyed and openmouthed at the girl who had spoken so boldly.

"It is true!" Rosalind went on recklessly. "I do not see why we must be paraded like merchandise on sale."

As she had warmed to her subject, her eyes sparkled with a burning light. She tossed her head again and set her curls to dancing.

Lady Mary found her voice at last. "Shame on you, brazen girl! Let no one hear you speak in such a manner! What is to become of you, tell me, if you fail to make at least a respectable match? And the sooner the better, although I have never before allowed myself to speak in such an uncharitable manner!"

She seemed about to burst into tears. Her mouth puckered and her eyelids trembled. With her small, plump hands clasped together, she raised her eyes to the ceiling as though praying that God would give her the strength to endure this burden.

Rosalind, regretting that she had thrown her aunt into such disorder, said, "But it is not necessary to have a gentleman's interest attached right away, is it? Corinna is already one-and-twenty and has been out three years. Yet you do not despair of her making an eligible match, dear aunt. She has had many offers, I know, although she does not boast of such."

"Corinna is different." In spite of the tightness of her mouth, Lady Mary's face softened with fondness. "Indeed she has had many suitors dangling after her since she left the schoolroom. You are not to compare yourself to her. Her portion is a generous one, and her background is all that it should be—after all, my father was an earl. And her beauty is such as to make her admired for many years to come. She claims she will marry no one whom she has not fallen in love with, but that, you may be sure, is simply a romantic notion and one of these days she will come to be sensible and choose the most eligible of her suitors, doing as she should, for there is not a beau among them all who, considering her fortune and her pretty manners and sweet disposition, although she is far from being hen-hearted . . ."

Having entangled herself in her own sentences, she stopped for a moment or two, and then said challengingly, "Surely you cannot deny that your cousin is a diamond of the first water!"

Neither of Corinna's cousins would deny that. Corinna Bannestock could be described as fairest of the fair, the most sought-after beauty in the entire city of London. Her curls were of raven-wing black, her dark eyes were warm and eloquent and her features were classically even.

At that moment, as her mother was singing her praises, they heard her voice, light and pretty as music, from the stairs, and there came a man's answering one, deep and rumbling.

Lady Mary hurried from the room, crying out endearments. A moment later the two entered the sewing chamber, and it was as though a great burst of sunshine had lightened this gloomy day.

Corinna was in her riding dress, its train thrown over her arm. Its colors became her—pale red with velvet piping of a darker shade. Her high-crowned hat had a scarlet feather which curled along its brim, and thus she was dressed in the very latest of equestrienne fashion.

She was stripping off her riding gloves as her mother trotted along beside her, fretting affectionately.

"Such an unpleasant day, my love. Are you certain you have not taken the chance of catching cold? It is so late in the afternoon, and I cannot understand why you must ride at this hour when it is not good *ton*. Surely you do not with to be thought out of the swim!"

Corinna made a tiny gesture as though to waft away such trivialities. As she crossed the threshold, her glance fell upon Rosalind, and her laughter chimed out like the pealing of little silver bells.

"Oh, Mama!" she gasped. "What are you doing to this

poor child? Certainly you have not planned for her to wear that!" and she fluttered her fingers in her cousin's direction. "Oh, truly, this is beyond anything! Not only would she be the laughing stock of the *ton,* but we, too, should be ruined if our friends see her in that—*that*—*!*"

"It is being made over, and when Biggers has finished with it," Lady Mary protested, "it will suit her well." She peered anxiously into her daughter's face, overset by the disapproval she saw there. "If you do not like it, I do not know what we shall do. I cannot ask your father for more money for Rosalind's clothing."

"No, indeed," Corinna agreed. "Certainly not when my wardrobe is full of gowns and pelisses and morning dresses, many of which I have not worn above two or three times."

She lifted a finger to her cheek, tilted her head and regarded Rosalind thoughtfully. Then she said, "There is the primrose crepe which I have not had on for three years, and then only once. I do not know why I took it in dislike, but I did, and now the color has come back into fashion and it will serve Cousin Rosalind well. Among all the pinks and whites and insipid colors, her gown would be a welcome relief. She shall wear my pearls and my Norwich scarf and do very well. Since we are almost equal in height, little change needs to be made. Jane, if you please, go upstairs and . . . No," she said, changing her mind. "Mama, you and I will do it. Perhaps we may find other things. After all this time," she said, regarding her mother's unwilling expression, "you may be sure that no one will remember anything I may have worn during my come-out season."

After the three had left the room and Harriet and Rosalind were alone, they exchanged troubled glances. Then the younger girl said with a sigh, "They mean to be kind. We must not lose sight of that. But, oh, Harry, how I wish that we were back in Sussex and that Papa were still alive! For I am sure I shall mislike the social world and be a flat failure." She put her hand over her mouth as soon as the words were out and her eyes took on a stricken look. "Oh, dear," she cried, her voice muffled. "I did not mean . . ."

"It is of no importance," Harriet said consolingly. "I know I have been a great disappointment to everyone. But to be forced to put on one's best clothes each night, to go from party to party and all the other social affairs, spending most of the evening trying to look as though it didn't matter that I was not asked to dance except by one or two gentlemen who felt sorry for me—well, I wished I had never had to come here!"

Rosalind ran to embrace her sister. "I never knew!" she cried, much distressed. "I knew you were not what they called 'all the crack,' but I thought there would be at least one gentleman who would aspire for your hand."

"But for you and Frederick," Harriet said, "I could not have endured it. Many times I have yearned to leave this house and find a post for myself somewhere—as a governess or a companion, perhaps."

"Do not ever think so again," Rosalind bade her fiercely. "I shall make sure there will be no need for that. When I make a respectable marriage, you shall remain with me. And Frederick, too. For we must make sure that Freddy has his opportunity. It is only through the generosity of Uncle Charles that he is being tutored for Oxford."

Her voice dwindled away, and their eyes met with the same stricken look. "Freddy!" Harriet said in a throbbing voice. "It cannot be, but, yes— At this very moment there is a young miss in a schoolroom somewhere who will one day become Freddy's wife."

They were silent for a little while as they contemplated the fate of this innocent and unaware child until Harriet finally said, "He has a few years in which to change."

Then they shook their heads. "Hopeless!" Rosalind murmured. "Poor Matthew! Such a job as he has tutoring Frederick! How he is able to stand it I cannot imagine. For that repellent little brat believes himself to know everything on every head, and it is difficult to see how anybody like that can be taught anything at all. But there!"

She reached over and patted her sister's hand. "We will not worry about that now. As for the other . . ."

She drew a deep breath and then her voice sounded more certain. "It matters not a whit if no one has offered for you yet. You are but nineteen, and I shall have plenty of time to find husbands for us both."

There was no response from Harriet, whose face seemed to have grown even bleaker. She appeared to be only half listening when Rosalind resumed speaking.

"Papa, if you will remember, often said that anybody could do anything if enough effort were expended."

Harriet gurgled a halfhearted laugh. "A fine example! Too bad that he did not expend more effort, and then we should not have lost the estate in Sussex."

"There is no sense," Rosalind said with a note of severity, "in crying over something that is over and done with. We must keep our minds of what is to come—eligible marriages for both of us."

"Do not put yourself in a pucker on my behalf," Harriet begged. "I do not mind if I dwindle into an old maid. For, you see, I am of the same mind as Corinna. I do not wish a marriage without love. I would prefer to have none at all."

Her face was mottled with a painful flush. "If I cannot have the man for whom I have a *tendre* . . ."

She lifted a hand quickly to her mouth, but it was too late. Rosalind cried, "Then there is some man to whom you are not indifferent! Oh, Harry, my dearest, someone has captured your fancy, and you have not told me so—or anyone else, I am persuaded—but borne it in silence. True, I have heard you sighing as you lay awake at night, but I thought it was only that you misliked this frightening city, or that Freddy had blue-deviled you. Now tell me, Harry, who is this man who is the cause of your unhappiness?"

Her sister shook her head. "That I will never do, for it is hopeless. He is far above my touch."

Rosalind regarded her gravely. "I cannot even guess who he might be, for you see close to no one at all, shut-

ting yourself away here, not even taking the stroll along
Bond Street of an afternoon, or riding out in the carriage
with Biggers or one of the footmen." She leaned forward
and peered into her sister's face as though answers would
come to her thus. "You do not see anyone—gentlemen,
that is—except Uncle Charles and Frederick's tutor, the
menservants, Corinna's suitors . . . !"

Harriet's blushes flamed even brighter. Her long, slender fingers were clenched into fists as they lay in her lap.
The words seemed to threaten to strangle her when she
said despairingly, "It does not matter, for he does not
know that I am alive, polite as he may be when we
chance to meet."

"Oh, Harry, my poor darling!" Rosalind took her sister
into her arms again. "How hen-witted I have been that I
could not see what was before my eyes! It was not that
you did not take when Aunt Mary launched you, for you
cared not a fig for that—but because this pea goose of a
man (yes, I shall call him that!) is too blind to see that
you are all good, all sweet, and that you would make him
a fine wife, even without a respectable portion. . . . For
our family, despite the fact that Papa was an unrepentant
gamester and died in Dun Territory, is of the best lineage,
going as far back as the Normans, he always said."

She paused for breath, and then, patting her sister's
drooping shoulder, she said, "Perhaps Aunt Mary will
have Biggers fashion a new gown for you, too, to wear at
my come-out ball. I shall do your hair myself, and you
know I am clever at that sort of thing. And when this
gentleman sees you fine as fivepiece . . ."

Harriet interrupted the bright chatter. "You are doing
it again, dear Roz. You are dreaming wild dreams which
will never come true. From head to toe I might be garbed
in fine silks and ermine, and he would not notice me except as Corinna's poor relation. For you see, best of all
sisters who even puts my happiness above her own, there
must have been countless other girls far more eligible and
pleasing to the eye than me who have been throwing their
handkerchiefs at him these dozen years. For he is what

they call 'a buck of the first cut,' the finest whip in London, as Freddy would say 'a bruising rider.' And he has a title and a great fortune and is related to earls and even a duke or two. Along with that, he is the most handsome and well-mannered of all Corinna's suitors."

She stopped, looking stricken, as she realized she had said too much, had revealed a secret that she had guarded carefully for long, lonely months.

"Do not notice it!" she begged. "Pay no attention to my silly prattle. It is nothing more than a childish notion!"

Rosalind had stepped away from her, slack-jawed and with her eyes round and glinting with something beyond astonishment, something very much like horror.

"Harriet Bannestock!" she cried, appalled. "You have fallen in love with the Nonpareil!"

2

Sir Julian Wickstead of Hammersland was grudgingly called by those who disliked him (of which there were a few) and his large circle of friends who admired him, an "out-and-outer." He was a Melton man, a skilled swordsman and pistol shot, and was able to hold his own in a bout of fisticuffs at Mr. Jackson's boxing saloon. He was an indifferent gamester, preferring the sports of the outdoors to confining himself to a gaming table at White's or Watier's.

Nature had been generous to him, too, for he was one of the most handsome men in all London, with the high-bridged nose of the true aristocrat, a strong and well-cut jaw, fine eyes which were the color of steel. If at times they wore a bored and weary expression, they could also become tender and gentle, especially with the large congregation of animals on his country estate. Children liked him because he had surprising patience with them, but few people saw that side of him. He could freeze a bore or a toady with a single glance, and mothers of hopeful daughters disliked him intensely because he refused to pay particular attention to their darlings.

He avoided the social scene as much as possible and was the despair of the patronesses of Almack's, refusing to enter its hallowed portals unless as a favor to a friend with an unprepossessing daughter who needed to be called attention to when she was fired off. At eight-and-twenty, he had been on the town for a decade, practicing his skill as an artful dodger when it came to being leg-shackled. But it had been thought that he was caught at last when he was often in the company of the enchanting Corinna Bannestock; and even the disappointed mamas and their daughters were forced to agree that the two would deal, for she was the nicest, as well as the most beautiful girl to have come upon the scene in many seasons, and he was the possessor of a great fortune and a proud name.

But nothing appeared to have progressed very far. Corinna had been out for three seasons and still was unable to make up her mind, it seemed.

Rosalind, awed by what her sister had revealed, cried, "But he is our cousin's suitor and has been ever since we have come into this house! Nearly three years he has been dangling after her. Surely you do not think . . ."

"I think nothing at all." Harriet wiped her eyes and sighed resignedly. "It does not matter, you see. He would never look at me in any case. I stood up with him at a ball last winter; he had asked me out of politeness, I am persuaded, my being Corinna's cousin. But when he comes to call upon her, and we chance to meet, it is as though he has never seen me before. Indeed, we have been introduced to each other no less than three times, and to him it is as though he were seeing me for the first time."

There was no bitterness in her voice, only a sad sort of acceptance. "If only Corinna would make up her mind! Either marry him or give him the mitten! You cannot dream how difficult it is to keep meeting him and knowing that I am invisible to him."

She could not hold back the tears, and Rosalind cried, in fierce anger, "Then he is blind indeed! He does not see your fine qualities, never complaining, never miffed. Shy as you are, what agony it must have caused you to be out on the marriage market, did it not?"

Harriet's bowed head gave her answer and Rosalind went on angrily, "I fear I am beginning to mislike exceedingly this nonesuch for having so little sensibility where you are concerned. I fear I shall not be able to treat him with civility when next we meet."

She was in deep thought for a few minutes, and then her eyes grew bright. "I know what I shall do; I shall snub him!"

Harriet said candidly, "He would not even notice if you were to do that."

Rosalind looked quelled, but only for a moment. "Perhaps you are right. No doubt other girls have tried that in order to fix his attention upon them. Then I shall have to come upon another way, and you may be sure that I shall! If it is Sir Julian you want, then I will see that you have him."

Her chin was set into a stubborn firmness, and her eyes seemed to flash fire. She was silent for a little while, then she began to mutter to herself. Harriet's face took on an expression of alarm.

"Oh, Roz, my dear love, what are you thinking? Please do not concoct one of your wild schemes. For it will only throw you into a scrape. Do you not remember Papa saying that you jumped before you looked and thus ended in a mud hole? Dearest, I wish you will not worry about me. I shall get over this notion soon."

She sounded so patient and resigned that Rosalind's heart began to ache, but her pity left no mark upon her determined, purposeful face.

"Do not ask me to do nothing. For I have just thought of the best of ideas to bring this coxcomb to his knees!" She clapped her hands in a childish gesture. "It will work, I am persuaded of that!"

A bright smile danced on her lips and in her eyes, and her curls bobbed as she nodded her head vigorously. "In no more than three weeks I shall be making my come-out.

Until then I shall avoid his lordship, make sure that he
and I do not meet." Harriet was about to speak but Rosalind held up a silencing hand. "Like you, I am not seen
by the baronet. He usually calls on Corinna only to escort
her to the theater or to balls or drums or other social affairs. He does not make formal visits."

"But what does that say to anything?" Harriet was
plainly bewildered. "I see no use in that."

"Because I have not finished telling you my plan. At
the ball Aunt Mary will hold for me, he will ask me to
dance, of course. Since I am a member of Corinna's
family, he will invite me to stand up with him. And
then . . ."

She drew a long, delighted breath. "I mean to flirt with
him and make him fall in love with me!"

She paused, waiting for her sister's approval of her
scheme, but Harriet shook her head and said quellingly,
"But you do not know how to flirt. And as to his falling
in love with you during just one dance, I vow that it happens so only in the romantic novels Aunt Mary says no
genteelly bred young woman should read."

"We shall accomplish nothing," Rosalind retorted, her
face and voice becoming severe, "if you keep raising ob-
jections. I shall have three weeks in which to practice
which, you must own, will be plenty of time."

For just an instant, she looked uncertain, but then her
spirits rose again and she mused, "True, there is no one
at hand for my purpose except Matthew, Freddy's tutor,
but perhaps Corinna will be having morning callers and
will not mind my joining them."

She looked into Harriet's puzzled face and went on
speaking more loudly and firmly. "You are wondering,
are you not, why I am set upon having Sir Julian attach
himself to me? Well, it is a very simple scheme to be sure.
He will fall in love with me, you see. Then when he offers
for me, I shall refuse him. He will be most set down and
humiliated, never believing that any woman would turn
the cold shoulder. Too, he will be heartbroken and will

need someone to restore his spirits, to comfort him. That will be you, Harriet!" she finished triumphantly.

Harriet's face had been changing from rosy pink to pasty white during the long monologue. Her voice sounded thin and unsteady as she cried, "Oh, Roz dearest, you cannot believe that I would be part of any flyaway scheme like that! It is by far quite the most foolish of your life. If it worked—and I will not take it, of course, that it would—then it would be most deceitful. To say nothing of its being cruel beyond anything!"

She saw with a sinking heart that nothing she could say would serve to influence her sister to change her mind, but she was determined to try, hopeless as the arguments might be, and was marshalling her thoughts when the other three women returned to the sewing chamber.

Biggers was carrying over her arm not one gown but three: the primrose crepe of which Corinna had spoken, one of palest yellow with a white satin underskirt, and a morning dress of green and ivory sprigged muslin.

In turn, Corinna took each dress from Biggers's arm and held it up, beaming at her cousin as she did so. "There! When Jane has made a few alterations, they will suit you well!"

She looked as happy as though their positions were reversed and it was she who was receiving new additions to her wardrobe. Rosalind felt a brief qualm. If only her cousin had been selfish or high in the instep, she'd have had no compunction about stealing one of her suitors, but Corinna had the sweetest of dispositions, a generosity far beyond what was called for, and she had never done a single mean deed to anyone in her life.

Then Rosalind glanced over at Harriet, and the drooping mouth and eyes dark with unhappiness strengthened her purpose again.

Later, when the two girls were in the bedroom they shared, Harriet once more tried to persuade her sister to abandon her scheme to ensnare Sir Julian, and then turn him over, heartbroken, to the other girl.

"But he and Corinna are not in love," Rosalind pointed out. "The times I have seen them together they acted more like brother and sister; they treat each other in a friendly way, not as a pair who are entangled in a romance. If, indeed, they were, they would have married any time these three years. No, my dear love, I shall have no need to blame myself if—I mean when—I attach him to me."

She glanced at the clock on the dresser made of undistinguished wood. The furnishings of the room were plain, not much more than those of a servant's room. But Rosalind and Harriet did not mind the lack of ornamentation, agreeing with their Aunt Mary's oft-repeated assertion that they were lucky "to have a roof over their heads."

Where else could they have gone, the two girls and their fifteen-year-old brother, if they had not been offered a home by their good-natured, warmhearted Uncle Charles?

His wife, from the start, had made it all too plain that she had no liking for the addition of three more to her household. Her hopes for restoring it to its former number rested upon making a match for Rosalind as soon as possible. An eligible *parti* must be found, one of respectable means. She had warned her husband's niece that she could not expect a title or a great fortune because of her own impecunious state. The good lady would have swooned had she been aware that Rosalind, for her sister, was setting her sights upon the greatest matrimonial prize in London.

Freddy, Rosalind knew with some uneasiness, was their greatest drawback. For who would wish to take into his household this odious fifteen-year-old?

No word was spoken that Freddy, from his great font of odds and ends of knowledge, did not contradict, challenge, or criticize. His tutor, Matthew Traynord (Freddy's sisters were wont to speak of him as "poor Matthew"), was a patient young man, much put upon, and an object of sympathy.

"Well, you cannot really blame Aunt Mary for wishing that we were somewhere else," Rosalind said in an effort to be fair. "I would not want Freddy around either if I had a choice."

Just as she finished speaking, there came a scratching at the door. Opening it she found one of the footmen with a message from Lady Bannestock. Her ladyship desired to see the two young ladies in the yellow drawing room. At once, the footman added, in a solemn voice.

They hurried about, bumping into each other as they both tried to see into the looking glass at the same time, fixing their curls, and shaking out their skirts.

They went downstairs in a great rush, for the yellow drawing room was used on special occasions. The same thought was in both their minds, that something ominous awaited them, and they shared a mutual feeling of excitement. There was also a shared feeling of uneasiness, and for Rosalind, a faint shadowing of guilt. She assured herself that Lady Mary couldn't know of her plan to ensnare Corinna's suitor for Harriet.

Minds could not be read.

But somehow the thought did not cheer Rosalind. She took Harriet's hand in her own as they reached the threshold of the drawing room. Certainly this must be an occasion of more than ordinary importance, for the entire family was gathered in front of the roaring fireplace.

3

Sir Charles, whose face usually wore an amiable expression, looked rather frighteningly solemn. Because of his girth, his height was not exceedingly noticeable, but on this March evening, with the logs in the fireplace snapping and hissing, and with the wind in the chimney making its own disturbing sound, he looked very much the master of the house.

His fine head, with its still-thick iron gray hair, was held in such a manner that even a stranger would know that he was a man of great consequence. His clothing was subdued but in the best of taste, his neckcloth arranged in a fashion not too elaborate, his knee breeches of a pleasing shade of blue, his stockings of cream color, and his waistcoat of many muted designs.

His lady, seated on a brocade-covered sofa, was looking up at him anxiously. Biggers had combed her hair in the new fashion which was too severe to be becoming to a woman of Lady Mary's age, for it revealed too much of her bulging forehead and did not completely cover her ears which were fairly prominent and too large for her face. Her undeniably handsome gown was of a not too

oppressing shade of purple, and she was wearing the
Bannestock diamonds, which were, Rosalind guessed, of
great value.

Corinna wore no jewelry with her pale green round
dress. Nor did she need any ornamentation, her eyes
being as bright as dark stars flashing in the firelight, and
her teeth as cleanly white as pearls.

Frederick Bannestock looked older than his fifteen
years, for he was almost as tall as the younger of his two
sisters. He was sprawled in an armchair at one side of the
fireplace. He did not rise as Rosalind and Harriet came
into the room. His only greeting was the raising of a lan-
guid hand, but they scarcely noticed his lack of civility
used as they were to it, and although Lady Mary often
pointed out to them his lack of polish, they were wont to
say that this was just Freddy's way and that his edges
would be smoothed off when he was in Oxford.

He gave promise of being a handsome young man once
he lost his youthful awkwardness. He had the same
sort of even features as Harriet and the blue eyes and
bright-colored hair of Rosalind. Unlike his sisters, however, his good looks were spoiled by a supercilious and
somewhat cynical expression unbecoming in one so
young.

Even with the lively fire in the hearth, Rosalind felt
herself shivering a little. The drawing room, furnished in
colors ranging from pale lemon to near orange, seemed
not to have the effect Lady Mary had hoped for it. Far
from giving the impression of eternal sunlight, it seemed
cold and insipid; and this room, her greatest decorating
failure, was usually closed off and used only on some
formal or important occasion as this family gathering por-
tended to be.

Sir Charles had in his hand, Rosalind saw, a small box
of polished wood which was fashioned in the shape of a
chest. There were small, exquisitely executed brass fittings
and a keyhole so tiny it could scarcely be seen. So carefully was Sir Charles holding it that he did not release a

hand to welcome the two girls, only gestured with his head to bring them all closer to him.

"Come, and you will see what I have been doing this day."

They all moved toward him obediently as he stood beside a graceful table with an inlaid mother-of-pearl surface. It was a strangely solemn moment, and Rosalind felt her heart begin to beat a little more rapidly. She held her breath as Sir Charles took from a pocket a miniature key. He looked at each of them in turn and then spoke in a grave voice.

"My dear family, you must know I have been busy these past weeks tending to my much-mourned mother's estate. All who knew her loved her, but it would be less than the truth to say that she was other than a fribble-dibble. Nothing was as it should have been, so careless was she about her possessions. Her man of business and I have both been in despair of ever disentangling her accounts—debts unpaid, cash and gold hidden in unlikely places, and her jewels, many of them of great value, in this place and that. We had a task, I may tell you, in straightening everything out."

He smiled finally, like a man from whose shoulders had been lifted a great burden.

"We shall keep Avernal, the estate in Bramington, for summer visits, at least for a while, but there will be little cash left when the obligations are paid. Her jewelry will go to you, my love," he told his wife. "The better part of it, that is, and to Corinna. And perhaps," he said with a kindly smile to his nieces, "we shall find some trinkets for you, too."

The thought popped into Rosalind's mind that since her father and Uncle Charles had been brothers and their mother her own grandmother, even one she had scarcely known, she and Harriet and Frederick should share in any inheritance.

But she could not say that aloud. For had not Uncle Charles been generosity itself and never so much as hinted, by word or raised eyebrows, that the three were

objects of charity? Or treated them any differently than
his own daughter? Too, he had been the eldest son, the
heir to the title, and there had been a long estrangement
between the younger brother and his mother.

Sir Charles placed the little box on the table beside him
and, with a little flourish, unlocked it and lifted the lid. At
first all Rosalind could see was a jumble of brightly
colored objects: a thin diamond chain with a topaz pendant like a huge, golden teardrop, a pair of ruby ear bobs,
a sapphire brooch, a bracelet of Florentine gold and
enamel. Then Sir Charles lifted out, with utmost care, a
little article. As it came into view, the women gathered
more closely around the table, and there was a sigh in
chorus. Even Freddy was heard to gasp.

It was the most exquisite object Rosalind had ever
seen, a tiny pin in the shape of a rose, its petals fashioned
of a delicate pink, shell-like substance glowing translu-
cently. There were six of the petals and upon each one
was a tiny, perfect diamond like a drop of dew. In the
heart of the rose was a very much larger diamond which,
in itself, seemed to Rosalind's dazzled eyes to be of value
beyond reckoning.

Beaming at his daughter, Sir Charles said, "It is to be
yours, my love. Your grandmother left no will but I am
sure, had she done so, she would have bequeathed it to
you. For she spoke often of your beauty, comparing it to
a rose."

Rosalind's lips opened, and then fell shut again. But
her eyes glinted with the unsaid words. This was not noticed by the others who were so fascinated by the beautiful little object that they were not aware of anything else.
She had been about to say that although Corinna was the
eldest girl in the family, custom had decreed that anyone
who wore any form of "Rose" in her name became, generation after generation, the possessor of the priceless pin.

Her father had so informed her, admitting frankly that
he had bestowed her name upon her for that reason. And
while she knew of the estrangement between him and his
mother during the last years of his life (so displeased had

she been about his gambling losses and the encumbering of his estate) Rosalind felt sure that her grandmother, had she settled her affairs before her death, would have bequeathed the valuable piece of jewelry to her.

For her own name had been Rosina. And before her there had been Rosanne and Rosella, down through the years, all of them noblewomen and the ancestors of the girl who stood silent and hurt.

Lady Mary, her eyes bright and greedy, tittered, "Oh, Corinna, my dear love, how beautiful this will look on your new gowns! You will be the envy of all London, I vow! I can barely wait until the night of Rosalind's come-out ball. You shall wear it then and later, of course, to Almack's. I can see the faces of Lady Jersey and Caroline Lamb who believe they are all the crack but have never owned such a stunning piece of jewelry. And as for Lucretia Fairlake! Well, she may be my bosom bow but I do not hesitate to say that she has always tried to out-do me in all things, and she will be green with envy for she believes her collection of jewelry to outshine all others." She drew a deep, delighted sigh. "You will be the talk of the *ton* for months to come."

The glances of Rosalind and Harriet met. The younger girl gave a quick shake of her head. She stiffened with alarm when Freddy began to speak. He had no interest in family heirlooms, considering such things frivolous and far beneath his touch, so no one was surprised when he said loftily, "Ninety-five percent of all diamonds come from South Africa where there are mines. The value of that little geegaw is, I should think, somewhere around ten thousand pounds. Do you know how much food that would buy for the poor wretches who work in the coal pits for starvation wages? And the ragged little waifs one sees wandering, homeless, about the streets? And those worse the wear for drink lying in the gutters with vermin crawling over them?"

He drew a long breath and was about to continue with his tirade, but his uncle said, "Enough! A gentleman does not speak of such matters in the presence of ladies. You are not in Parliament, you know!"

His face had lost its good-humored expression, and he stared at his nephew with disfavor. "We will have no more speeches from you, Frederick. We have more than enough so-called leaders with radical ideas. You will beg the pardon of the ladies, then after dinner you will find your tutor and do a little extra studying. Which will, I fear, be more punishment for your tutor than for yourself," he added dryly.

He turned to his wife. "I do wonder if Matthew Traynord was a good choice for teaching this young sprig. I fear Frederick may be getting his strange notions from that quarter."

"Oh, no, that cannot be so!"

It was Rosalind who spoke although Harriet, too, had opened her mouth in defense of Freddy's tutor. Then she closed it hastily, blushing.

"Dear Uncle Charles," Rosalind pleaded, "you must not worry yourself on that head. Freddy's notions are his own. On all matters Matthew feels just as he should. He is a most sensible young man . . ."

She broke off when she became aware that the others were regarding her in a very peculiar manner, having been taken aback by her vehement praise of Matthew Traynord.

"Pray forgive me," she said to Lady Mary. "It was ungenteel of me to speak in such a loud voice. But we have had so many tutors, and all of them have resigned their post because they were making no headway with Freddy who," and she cast a despairing glance at him, "seems to feel that he needs no teaching since he knows everything about all things already."

There appeared in her brother's eyes a glitter that bespoke the beginning of a quarrel, but his lordship held up a restraining hand. "We will not discuss this now, if you please." Then turning to his wife, he said, "I shall lock Mama's jewelry in the safe box in the desk in my chamber and put the key in one of the drawers. Then, should you and the girls wish to bedeck yourselves with one piece or another when I am away, it will be available to you, my dear. There is a great deal of value here and we must guard it well." He sighed deeply. "You cannot know what a great relief it is to have these things at last safely in my hands!"

"Indeed, sir, I can well imagine, and your bravery is to be much admired. The road to Brighton is not a place where one can feel safe these days. Not with highwaymen lurking in wait for travelers. Not above three days past Lucretia was telling me of a post chaise which was halted and its passengers robbed of all their possessions!"

She pressed her plump little hands against her bosom, looking so distressed that her daughter and Sir Charles fluttered about her trying to comfort her. Whether or not it was play-acting Rosalind could not tell, but only that afternoon Lady Mary had lectured her nieces on the expediency of praise and admiration as a means of pleasing gentlemen. Now her point seemed to have been well taken, for Sir Charles was on one knee beside his lady's chair, patting her hand and promising that he would never again set forth on a long journey without his driver and postillions well armed.

Freddy was watching the little scene with a sardonic half smile. Rosalind could feel no annoyance with him for she was entertaining the same sort of suspicion that, as Freddy would have said, the lady was doing it much too brown.

Nothing more was said that evening about the heirloom jewelry. (Lady Mary, who had never known the lack of anything she wanted or needed in her entire life, was wont to say that too much concern with possessions was vulgar.) But in the bedroom they shared, her two nieces talked of it.

"It should belong to you," Harriet said, her voice still soft and with only a flush of indignation revealing her true feelings. "I was forced to bite my tongue lest I say so to Uncle Charles. Oh, my dearest sister, it grows harder each day for us to be happy here. Lady Mary has done her best with me, and it was not her fault if I did not take. Now it is your turn, and she will try to find an eligible *parti* for you."

But not for an unselfish reason, Rosalind told herself silently. She is hoping someone will form a partiality and take us off her hands.

"I doubt not," Harriet said, casting a fond glance at the other girl, "that you will have many offers. But if it happens that there is no one you have a fancy for, perhaps we might leave here and find positions somewhere. You have said yourself that I am an accomplished seamstress and you paint in water colors with a deal of talent . . ."

"We shall speak no more on this head," Rosalind said firmly. "I know what I must do and how to do it."

"Yes," said her sister, much subdued. "I am sure you have spoken the truth."

4

For the next three weeks, Sir Charles Bannestock's household was in turmoil. Window draperies were taken down and replaced. Carpets were pulled up and cleaned. Furniture was moved from one place to another so that the unhappy gentleman was often forced to look from room to room for his favorite chair.

Footmen were fitted for new livery and were allowed to purchase new powdered wigs. Housemaids sewed late into the night on new aprons and caps, and then rose early in the morning to scrub upon their knees every exposed inch of woodwork and floor.

Small crises arose. Her ladyship, having set her heart on having the ballroom draped, tent-fashion, in pink satin, was sent the wrong shade of the color and immediately went into hysterics.

The problem was solved by Sir Charles, who suggested great bouquets of flowers tied with gold ribbon to match the ballroom's small, gold chairs which had been newly painted.

Lady Mary fell into the habit of wandering about the house muttering to herself such words as, "supper room

. . . tables for the card players . . . not too many
waltzes . . ."

Fortunately her husband and daughter were cool in the
face of the chaos having already suffered through these
preparations for the come-out ball; they were repetitions
of Corinna's and Harriet's launching into society, the
strain of which threatened to fell her with vapors and
frazzled nerves.

Nor did these frantic activities reassure Rosalind who,
while scornful of the whole affair and its significance,
prayed that she would not disappoint the woman to whom
the admiration and envy of her friends was so important.

She saw Lady Mary examining again and again her
guest list, muttering worriedly to herself that she might
have inadvertently omitted someone of consequence from
it. It seemed to Rosalind, who had seen the awesome
stack of invitations before they were delivered, that there
could not have been anyone of importance ignored. Lady
Mary said in answer to that remark that yes, she expected the ball would be the veriest of squeezes; and that,
quite plainly, was what she desired above all things.

Sketchy meals were served on the day of the ball. In
answer to Freddy's grumbling (for, beyond prosing, the
thing he liked best of all was eating) her ladyship pointed
out that supper would be served later in the evening, and
there would be no one attending the festivity who would
be able to say that she was a nip squeeze in the matter of
food served at her parties.

Freddy had protested, too, about attending the ball. In
ringing accents of contempt, he condemned all such social
affairs as time-wasting and disgracefully extravagant,
money spent to no good purpose. His uncle put a period
to such talk by saying, "You will add nothing to the company, I fear. But it will be well for you to know that a
gentleman has certain obligations to his name and station.
You must learn to take with good grace the duties which
may, at the time, seem repellent to you."

He turned to Matthew Traynord, Freddy's tutor, who
had also been summoned to his lordship's book room. "It

is milady's wish that you, too, be present. It seems that there are never enough unattached young men to supply the ladies with dance partners. I believe she has in mind for you to give your attention to the less attractive young ladies who otherwise would not be asked to dance. Wallflowers, I believe they are called."

He ended with a man-to-man smile and clipped the man on his shoulder, unaware of Matthew's dull flush and reddened ears.

Freddy's tutor was tall to the point of being ungainly. He had straight, pale-brown hair and features so large they did not seem to match his long, thin face. His Adam's apple was prominent, and he would have been called far from handsome except that he had kind eyes of a pleasing shade of gray.

He was an excellent educationist and was awaiting a post as a schoolmaster, but in the Bannestock household he found himself no more than a cut above the servants and not, of course, of a class of his employer. Freddy was a challenge to him. Much as he disliked and disapproved of the boy's radical notions, he tried with all conscientiousness to drum into that stubborn young head the knowledge that would gain him entrance to Oxford.

On the night of the ball, Rosalind and Harriet made their toilette together. Not for them were Biggers' ministrations, nor were they helped by any of the housemaids, who were busy with last-minute chores. Nor would they have favored having strangers in their chamber on that most important of nights for both, in spite of themselves, were somewhat overset at the prospect of facing the leaders of the *ton* who would be arriving at any minute.

When they had finished dressing, they studied each other soberly. Rosalind was wearing the primrose crepe which had been Corinna's three years ago and was now lightly disguised by rosette-shaped pearl buttons down its length and a cluster of them at the throat. It hung straight and graceful with a half-train in the back and a Norwich scarf was flung over her shoulders. With long white gloves

pulled tightly over her elbows and a single glittering orna-
ment in her hair, she looked, Harriet said admiringly,
"fine as five piece."

Harriet's own gown was of pale blue lace over an underskirt of deeper blue. She wore matching kid slippers
and carried a white silk fan. She looked sweet and sensible, and while not the striking figure her sister made, she
was uncommonly well-looking and Rosalind hoped fervently that for once Harriet would make a splash and attach to herself some interested gentleman who might
cause jealousy in the heart of Sir Julian Wickstead.

She started guiltily as Corinna scratched at the door
and then came into the room. Both girls, for a moment,
stared silently at their cousin, quite struck dumb by her
awesome beauty. She was wearing a favorite shade of
green with small, puffed sleeves and a high waist that ac-
cented her curved, slim figure. Around her neck was the
topaz pendant on its diamond chain and no other jewelry
except diamond bracelets on her gloved arms.

She was carrying a posy which she held out to Rosalind. "For you. It was delivered just now. It is," she
said with a deep curtsy, "special. You have been well favored this night, my dear. It is from Prinny."

Rosalind looked at her blankly and then drew in her
breath when Corinna said, "The Prince of Wales, of
course. He will not be able to attend—he did not for my
come-out, either—but he is an old friend of Papa's and
this is the way he expresses his good wishes."

Both Rosalind and Harriet were speechless, and into
that silence their cousin said, with a change of mood,
"You are not to bother your head about anything tonight,
dear Roz. You will be a great success, of that I am persuaded. I am only sorry . . ."

She hesitated and seemed to be at a loss for a moment
or two. Then she said in a quiet, earnest voice, "I have
been meaning to speak to you for these past three weeks
about the pin which Papa wished me to have—the rose
pin that belonged to Grandmamma. I know it was your
expectation that it belong to you. But I did not wish to

speak on that head for Papa at that time was perturbed with all the duties that were left to him in settling the estate."

She touched the bodice of her gown. "As you can see, I am not wearing it this night. If Mama speaks of it I will put her off; I will tell her I had a wish to wear this dress and it would not match. Rosalind, dear cousin, if nothing else—if she will not consent to letting me bestow it upon you, perhaps we can share it."

Rosalind felt a sudden hot film speed across her eyes. How sweet a nature had this lovely girl, her inner self as beautiful as her face and body. "You are too good, too kind," she choked. "Indeed the pin is as nothing to me!"

"No, indeed, for nothing could improve you this minute." Corinna smiled her enchanting smile. "Now come along," and she stretched a hand to each of them. "It is time to go downstairs, for already I hear a carriage arriving. Mama will want you with her at the head of the stairs to greet your guests."

Lady Mary was a majestic figure in a towering turban, made even more imposing with tall, stiff feathers above her forehead, which matched her purple gown. Nodding, smiling, extending her hand, she evinced no nervousness over the success of her endeavor to launch her niece into the social swim.

Rosalind was awed by the steady stream of guests, their number increasing as the hour wore on, all of whom were dressed to the nines, the women in the latest fashion of gowns and coiffures, bedecked with jewelry, the men in evening clothes and wearing fobs and seals and diamond studs in their neckpieces.

Rosalind heard names of great consequence, many titles, some borne by those close to the throne. Aunt Mary, she thought with relief, must be well satisfied with the evening's work. With the floor of the ballroom filled with dancers, card playing in the smaller rooms and some mild gambling being carried on in his lordship's book room, it might be honestly said that this was indeed a squeeze.

Lady Mary dismissed her niece at eleven o'clock and waved her toward the ballroom. "No more than two dances with a gentleman," she warned. "To show more partiality for any partner is not the thing."

Nervously, Rosalind edged through the onlookers at the rim of the ballroom floor, most of whom were young men gazing at the scene with critical eyes, and was immediately claimed for a dance. At once her uneasiness fled, for her partner was skilled in the waltz, leading her surely in the whirling steps, slowing down before she was completely breathless.

Looking about her she saw Harriet dancing with Matthew Traynord, and Corinna with a young officer in his regimentals who looked both handsome and bemused. It was Sir Julian Wickstead for whom Rosalind was searching in the crowd, but when she saw him, her only feeling was of dismay.

His partner was Genivera, Lady Benedict, the most notorious, flirtatious, outrageously mannered care-for-nothing in the whole of London. Only her title and the great fortune of Lord Benedict kept her from being an outcast from polite society. Even knowing as little as she did about such affairs, in this case Rosalind had heard gossip in the drawing rooms upstairs and the servants' quarters downstairs. One of the maids had smuggled in a newspaper which featured scandalous tidbits and Rosalind had learned all the seamy, shocking activities of the Lady Benedict. To find her in the arms of the man whom Rosalind had chosen for her sister threatened to throw her into disorder.

Corinna, with her sweetness of disposition and amiable ways, could be easily manipulated into losing her suitor. But Lady Benedict, who had bold, black eyes, a provocative smile and a compliant husband, would know all the tricks of holding on to a man she loved and would be certain to throw a spoke into the wheels of Rosalind's scheme.

5

Throughout the evening Rosalind was aware of Lady Mary's frequent glances upon her. There could be no question of her failing to "take," for the young men flocked about her clamoring to be her partner and paying her pretty compliments, none of their faces and names remembered more than a few minutes after they passed out of sight.

It was while she was dancing with Sir Willton Turncroft that her aunt's smug expression changed to anxiety. That she disliked the young baronet's presence as a guest in her house was plain enough in her pursed lips and rapidly blinking eyelids.

Sir Willton had been guilty of the discourtesy of arriving after eleven o'clock. He had sauntered about for a few minutes, ogling the young women before he chose, with an arrogant sort of bow, her ladyship's niece as his partner. He had not danced with anyone else and was not even content with the two waltzes she allotted him, being guilty of the breech of etiquette of asking her for a third dance.

She had refused, not at all comfortable in his presence,

for she had never before been in the company of a man of his ilk; the bold gaze of his eyes, so dark brown they were almost black, the extravagant speech and cynical manner caused a tingling of her nerves which was not at all pleasant.

Too, she had heard Lady Mary discussing him one evening with her husband, and nothing that had been said about him had been fit for young ears, her ladyship said rapidly breaking off the conversation when she realized that she was being overheard.

What Rosalind learned, though sketchy, was enough to both intrigue and disgust her. Sir Willton was a rake—although that would not have barred him from polite company—but he, albeit still but four-and-twenty years of age, had already been embroiled in a gaming argument which had led him to being called out in a duel during which his opponent had been slain. Too, there had been a scandal involving a married woman, he was known to be ugly natured when drinking, his servants had whispered stories about orgies at his estate in Hertfordshire.

He had not waited for an invitation to the ball; claiming a distant relationship with Lady Mary, he had sauntered in at his own convenience causing the good lady to be much overset by his presence, hoping fervently that Rosalind, to whom he seemed to have taken a fancy, would not be guilty of the mistake of going in to supper with this notorious buck.

Rosalind had no such intention. Escorting her from the floor, Sir Willton inadvertently touched the arm of Wickstead, who whirled about and favored Rosalind with a smile which showed much pleasure.

"At last," he said in a self-congratulatory way, "I find myself close enough to request the pleasure of a dance. What a bit of luck! I was beginning to fear that I should not have the opportunity."

Sir Willton stood glowering, seeming to wish to protest but much quelled by the taller, more solidly built young nobleman whose consequence was greater than his own.

As they squeezed their way to the place where a new

set was forming, Sir Julian spoke words which brought a little shine of excitement to her eyes and a flush to her cheeks.

"I am persuaded that Sir Charles and Lady Mary must be proud this night. Never have I seen any one young lady like yourself make a more successful come-out. I am, in fact at this moment, the envy of a deal of young bucks who would gladly change positions with me, if they could."

The evening had been one of enchantment for Rosalind. She had been complimented on her gown by no one less than Lady Jersey; she had been offered vouchers to Almack's by the formidable duchess of Tennysworth. She had never once been left without a partner. But this was above everything—the way Sir Julian had spoken in an easy, amiable fashion and yet with a certain ring of truth.

And then she suddenly grew cold, her face set in haughty lines, a remote expression coming into her eyes. For she had just remembered that she was not supposed to be smiling up into his face, thanking him silently for his kindness which had seemed to go beyond common civility. Her plan had been to snub him, to bewilder him with contempt and so arouse his interest to such a degree that Harriet—with her sweetness and sympathy—would, when she next came into his view, find him needing someone like her to mend his bruised sensibilities.

So Rosalind did not reply to those words which had sent her spirits up into the treetops for a little while. As they faced each other in their places for the country dance, she kept a very disparaging expression on her face and refused to let her eyes meet his.

For a moment or two, he did look bewildered. His fine eyebrows drew together as he wondered about the change in this engaging young miss. When he had happened to meet her at Sir Charles's house, she had not exactly passed his notice but he had not seen her as anything except Corinna Bannestock's young cousin who was not long out of the schoolroom and merely another pretty young miss.

Now why was she keeping her chin up in that strange manner? The whole thing became even more confusing a moment later. For Rosalind, on her way down the aisle between the dancers, suddenly remembered something. It came to her in a burst of realization that this was not the way she should be acting toward Sir Julian at all. She was using the wrong tactics. For while her first plan had been to snub him, she had discarded that scheme in favor of making him fall in love with her! Immediately she forced her face into a provocative smile, and when they met again in the figures of the dance, her eyelids were blinking and her head tossed flirtatiously.

What, Sir Julian wondered, was the matter with the idiotish child? One moment she had acted as though she was hard put to endure his company, and the next she was posturing and gesturing like the veriest street dowd; albeit one who had taken almost complete leave of her senses.

The dance ended mercifully, and Sir Julian escorted his partner to her aunt and her sister, the latter, too, in some sort of incomprehensible state, dropping her head and flushing as he spoke to her out of civility. She seemed to have no voice—or else no wits and he wondered if there was not a strange strain on their side of the family—for she made no reply to his greeting. The pair of them were, at least, out of the ordinary breed of females who, even at that moment, would have been overcome with pleasure had he paid them as much attention as he was bestowing upon these two Bannestock cousins.

If that bespoke conceit he was not to be too severely blamed. He had been spoiled since infancy and as a bonny child indulged by nursemaids, governesses, servants and his doting female relatives. Then, when he went out upon the town, he had been pursued by young ladies and their mamas, handkerchiefs had fallen steadily at his feet, all sorts of tricks and plots to ensnare him had been tried and resulted in failure.

He was in no hurry to marry although he sometimes

felt the touch of loneliness which often is the bane of those of nonesuch attributes. Bored at times, he was grateful when there came into his ken something new and different; he was intrigued by Corinna's cousins and made a mental note to send them both posies in the morning.

On that morning, the Bannestock ladies arose late and were not receiving visitors until well after eleven o'clock. They met then at the breakfast table and indulged in that most pleasant of diversions—talking over the festivities of the night before.

Lady Mary said, with great satisfaction, that the come-out ball could be counted a great success, a veritable "squeeze," with all the members of the best society in attendance. "And you, and you, too, Harriet, behaved exactly as was called for," she said to her niece, "although I was not pleased with the particular attention Willton Turncroft was paying to you. We must be civil to him if he calls." Her gaze swept around the circle of faces and came to rest upon Corinna's. "My love, you, too, were quite the most admired, but that, of course, is an old story. But there is one thing I do not understand. Why did you not wear the rose pin? I noticed last night you were not doing so, but had no chance to speak of it then."

Corinna said carelessly, "The color, Mama. It did not match my dress. It will never be, I think, my favorite piece of jewelry."

"Do not say so!" Lady Mary appeared to be quite distressed. "It is of great value and quite the only piece of its kind. I particularly wanted to have Lucretia see it for although she is my closest bosom bow, I must confess that she is of an acquisitive nature and is never so happy as when she is able to bring into view something which she possesses and I do not." She made a vague little gesture with her plump, white hand. As though, Rosalind thought, disclaiming the lack of charity in her words. "I am, of course, most fond of Lucretia but I should be guilty of a monstrous lie if I said I did not find her at times boring."

She helped herself to another slice of bread and sighed. "Fortunately I did not see so much of her last night, being busy with other things. Had I not been so occupied, I am sure I should have been forced to listen to her complaints about her servants, her children who are long since married, and—most of all—her mother-in-law, Isabel, the Dowager Countess of Fairlake who, it does seem, keeps poor Lucretia and the rest of her family in an uproar because of her eccentric actions. I do not know how poor Lucretia stands it."

Rosalind was not listening attentively to this confusing monologue. Aunt Mary did not seem to be able to decide whether she was in or out of sympathy with her friend, and so her niece turned her thoughts in another direction.

The mail had arrived and been exclaimed over by Lady Mary. Never, she declared, well-pleased, had there come into her house so many cards of invitation to be placed on the fireplace mantel.

"I make no doubt that it will be a season to remember—routs, balls, drums—to say nothing of the bids there will be to the theater parties, concerts, and Venetian breakfasts. You will do very well, my dear."

She smiled her smug little smile at Rosalind, who wondered why the woman so consistently ignored Harriet, speaking past her or around her, when it was the elder of the two sisters who needed reassurance and a little kindly attention.

"You will, I am certain, find yourself quite a respectable success."

Indifference was all Rosalind felt about such matters at that moment. Not only was Harriet drooping over her breakfast and eating little of it but Corinna, too, usually of such a sunny disposition, seemed to be in peculiarly low spirits. She had glanced through the mail when her mother had finished poring over it and then pushed it aside. What, Rosalind wondered, was there which had caused the girl to be blue-deviled? At the ball last night, she had been much sought-after, never lacking a partner, surrounded between dances by those bucks known as tulips of the *ton,* beamed upon by their hopeful mothers.

Even Frederick, scornful as he was of such frivolous matters, had been heard to say that his cousin had looked "slap up to the echo" and Matthew Traynord, his tutor, had blushingly paid her a compliment in politer terms.

(Freddy, arms folded and with a dark scowl on his face, had stood leaning against a wall, eschewing whatever diversion he might have found by mingling with guests, until supper was announced. Then he made a dash to the refreshment tables like someone who had not partaken of food for many long hours. Sir Charles had been heard to say dryly that the reason Freddy's sympathies lay with those suffering hunger pains was that he knew its pangs so often.)

Morning visitors that day included Lucretia, Lady Fairlake, as Lady Mary had known beforehand she would be—full of complaints about her mother-in-law and various household annoyances.

She was repining her way to the door when Haybolt, the butler, admitted Sir Willton Turncroft who refused to be announced. This threw her ladyship into sad disorder for not only did she consider him no fit man to consort with her three well-bred, innocent young ladies, but he had come to call in his riding clothes and so was guilty of flagrant solecism.

He did not seem to notice the coolness of her manner. He set about to entertain the others with clever remarks, some of them so scandalous they should not have been repeated in polite company. He had special smiles for Corinna, calling her "cousin" and paying her lavish compliments, and Rosalind suspected that he might be hanging out for a rich wife. She was, however, disabused on that head when finally Sir Willton took his leave.

Lady Mary said grudgingly that he could not be counted a fortune hunter having been left a sizable fortune by his father. "And," she said in an effort to be just, "that is to his credit, his having increased it. But there is so much more about him which I cannot like."

Rosalind, her forehead puckered, asked, "But why is it so otherwise for a woman?"

"I don't, I fear, understand what it is you are trying to say." Lady Mary, too, was frowning. "I find no sense in your words."

"It is just that things are not the same for us and them."

The eyes of the other three were gazing at her, those of Corinna and her mother curious, Harriet beginning to look uneasy as though she was fearing that Rosalind would embark upon one of her disturbing statements. She raised a hand in warning but her sister did not heed it but went on speaking earnestly.

"If one of us should capture the interest of a wealthy gentleman and receive an offer from him, it would be a cause of great rejoicing for her mama and the envy of her friends. That is why we are presented to society, so that we may find an eligible husband. On the other hand, a man who is thin in the pocket and tries to fix his interest upon a lady of means is counted as a fortune hunter and is regarded with contempt by all who know him."

Lady Mary's cheeks swelled as though they were full of words she could not force out. Her eyes blinked rapidly, but she was spared an answer to Rosalind's oration by Haybolt's announcing that Sir Julian Wickstead had arrived.

Something rather strange happened to Miss Rosalind Bannestock in that moment. Her heart gave a little leap, and she knew that this was what she had been waiting for all morning.

6

Trailing along behind Sir Julian was a footman carry-
ing three posies, one for each of the young ladies, and a
larger bouquet for Lady Mary. These he presented with
the utmost grace, waving away expressions of gratitude
with a disclaiming gesture. That the gentleman not only
was well versed in the rules of etiquette and good *ton* but
was also a naturally kind and generous man was quite
evident. It was entirely plain, too, that Lady Mary, while
not a matchmaking mama since there had never been need
for her to be so with her much sought-after daughter,
favored Sir Julian as a suitor for Corinna's hand. She
beamed benevolently upon him, urging him to remain
long enough to partake of refreshments.

Rosalind found his presence disturbing, remembering
the sad botch she had made of her opportunity to ensnare
him the night before. She was aware of his long, rather
puzzled stare and could meet his eyes only briefly. She
mumbled her pretty speech of thanks without looking at
him, transferring her attention to Harriet whose blushes,
she feared, were much too revealing.

What a pair of hen-witted females he must think us! she told herself. What a relief it must have been for him to find the fair Corinna able to carry on the conversation in a sensible manner!

After a few minutes of chitchat, Lady Mary left the room, signaling to her two nieces to follow her.

When they were well out of earshot of the pair in the drawing room, she said, her face aglow, "While it is not my custom to encourage gentlemen to be entertained by a young lady alone, it is different in this case. Sir Julian, I am persuaded, has it in his mind to offer for Corinna before too much time has passed. Both her father and I approve of the match and I have no doubt that he will speak to us, perhaps even today, about marriage settlements. He is the catch of the town, of course, and the only suitor she has had who is worthy of her. There was a time, three years ago . . ."

She paused, her face growing a little troubled. Then, shaking her head as though to rid it of troublesome thought, she said, "But there! It was long ago and done with and buried."

But Sir Julian did not offer marriage that day. Rosalind, in search of her embroidery which she had laid down somewhere when she had been overset by the presence of Sir Julian and could not find, came across the two again as they stood by the entrance door. The man, his hat and gloves in hand, was saying something to Corinna which Rosalind guessed was of a soothing nature if one were to judge by his murmuring voice and sympathetic gaze.

But what could it be? True, Corinna had seemed to be blue-deviled since she had arisen that day, and that in itself was exceedingly strange, and Rosalind began to feel alarmed. Then the good-byes were said, and Corinna turned back to the hall, her face now calm and quiet, her mood evidently lightened.

In the days that followed, nothing of any importance was said about the two whose betrothal seemed imminent on that day after Rosalind's come-out. No more was mentioned about marriage settlements, Corinna's good spirits revived, not only Sir Julian but many other young men paid her court. She was known to have had at least three offers, all of which she refused but which gave Lady Mary cause for boasting.

But even though nothing of a serious nature developed between Corinna and Sir Julian, Rosalind's scheme reached no success. Whenever she and Sir Julian met, it was invariably in the presence of others. Now and then he dropped in at Almack's, stayed long enough to stand up with Corinna or chat with the hostesses. On the rare occasions he danced with Rosalind he dutifully chose Harriet, too, as his partner for the following set, casting that maiden into a state of tongue-tied blushes.

Rosalind did not lack for suitors although none of them, even though she was determined to form no attachments until Harriet's future was assured, could she take seriously.

Sir Willton Turncroft was particular in his attentions. He was not a man to be discouraged, seeming to be amused by Lady Mary's quite evident disapproval of him. Again she warned Rosalind about encouraging him. "For all that he belongs to my family—although, thank God it is a very faint connection—he is not one I can feel easily with even in my own home." Her forehead was creased with the effort of thinking. "I do not know why that is so, only that he disturbs me. Is there not any other," she asked hopefully, "who has taken your fancy? Sir Henry Hargrove perhaps?"

Rosalind pointed out that Sir Henry was old enough to be her father with a few years left over. "And he is grossly fat and snuffles in a most disgusting way. And," she went on hurriedly, knowing that Aunt Mary would list all the gentlemen who had called upon her or sent posies and trinkets, thus making her feel guilty for having rejected matrimonial prospects, "Lord Arndale has already had two wives, Bertram Sindclair is a hopeless gamester, Sir

Dyson has a dragon of a mother who expects him to make a remarkable match with an heiress."

She did not mention the man who had developed such a *tendre* for her that she was thrown into the greatest discomfort. She felt the utmost pity for Matthew Traynord, Freddy's tutor, recognizing the signs of a man in love: the trouble he had in speaking to her in an unexceptional manner, the flushes when he was in her presence, the yearning in his eyes which followed her. It had started, she guessed, when he had seen her at the height of her good looks on the night of her come-out ball. She was thankful that no one but herself was aware of his secret feelings, not Freddy, who was so engrossed in his own concerns and plans for the future that he was unaware of what went on around him (Freddy, during those spring weeks, had decided to go into politics when his education was completed and was full of schemes to change the world); certainly not Sir Charles or his lady, to whom Matthew was no more than one hired out of their needs; not Corinna, who had regained her spirits and was caught up in the busy whirl of London in the season.

Only Harriet had divined the way the land lay. "Oh, poor Matthew! So in love he is with you! My dear sister, you must be kind to him, for I fear he suffers much. I wish, for his sake, that he might soon receive his appointment as a schoolmaster, for he will not recover from his pain while he is here in this house seeing you every day."

So absorbed was Rosalind in her determination to ensnare Sir Julian for her sister that she could see Matthew's unrequited *tendre* in an advantageous light. "Although I am most sorry for him," she said, "I do not see why he cannot be of use to us. I have thought often that if Sir Julian were to know that I am desirable to other gentlemen, he might see me in a different light. He must know that I am attractive to Arndale, Sindclair and Dyson, but is aware that I should never accept the handkerchief thrown at me by any of those gentlemen. Matthew is of a different cloth. Were in not for his lowly station, he would be welcomed everywhere. But that will change and I . . ."

"Rosalind!" Harriet cut in with unaccustomed warmth. "You are not to use Matthew in such a shabby manner. Does he not have enough on his plate trying to put knowledge into the head of our brother? I am surprised and saddened at your selfishness . . ."

She broke off suddenly and placed a hand across her mouth. Her face took on an appalled expression. "Oh, my dear love, how could I have spoken to you in such an unfriendly way? Do forgive me! It was only that I pity Matthew, so unhappy as he must be."

"And you are right," Rosalind said generously, "for I gave no thought to him at all except carelessly, and his life must needs be wretched. I must not include him in my plans. But . . ."

She put her hand against her cheek and tilted her head in a thoughtful manner. Within seconds her eyes had brightened. "To make Sir Julian jealous is the best of all ideas. But I was picturing it in my mind with the wrong man."

Her head began to nod vigorously. "I have not seen Wickstead and Turncroft together for over a few times. Yet I was persuaded that they did not have a liking for each other. I am sure Sir Julian knows of his unsavory past and disapproves of his visits here. If I allow Sir Willton to pay me particular attention, he is bound to notice me as he has not done very much so far," she said candidly.

Harriet would have argued against this further development of her sister's scheme and refused to endorse it. But having known Rosalind from babyhood, she was all too aware that it would be carried out, regardless of anything she might say.

From that moment on, Rosalind was often in Sir Willton's barouche. Lady Mary, after arguing futilely that no young lady of breeding would be seen in the company of a man of such reputation, permitted these excursions only

when accompanied by her sister, a maidservant, or—as
last resort—a footman. Rosalind was not of such consequence that she might have her own abigail and since
Harriet was reluctant to join the fashionable mode of conduct and be seen among the leaders of society, Lady
Mary had to lay down strict rules for her younger niece,
who chafed under them as she revealed to Lizzie, the
housemaid who most frequently was her chaperone.

Lizzie was an amiable young girl who had barely
reached the age of sixteen and who had few brains and an
overabundance of romantic notions. On a lowering day
when rain seemed imminent, Sir Willton drove his barouche with the two women in it twice around the park
and then he turned his horses in the direction of Kensing-
ton. He was a little abstracted; the ride was not a very
long one. When they were near Grosvenor Square, he
pulled up and, getting out of the carriage, motioned for
Lizzie to climb down. When Rosalind, puzzled, would
have left, too, he restrained her with a light touch on her
arm.

"The girl can walk back; it isn't so far. You and I, my
lovely Rose, will not need an abigail to join us in what we
are to do."

He was smiling down at her, his eyes animated by a
light which made her feel uncomfortable. "I shall see that
you are set down at your door when our little excursion is
over."

The excursion of which he spoke was, she learned, a
visit to his own house in St. James Square. "I have only
this very week had it all redecorated. I should like to have
your opinion on whether or not it is attractive to the female eye."

Since the redecorating was already finished, Rosalind
could see no point in anyone giving an opinion on the
completed product. Too, she had not the slightest intention of visiting a young man in his home, still afternoon
that it might be. Too vividly her imagination could see
Lady Mary's expression of horror that such a ramshackle
course of action had been even suggested to her.

"Come now," Sir Willton was saying in a cynically amused way, "what makes you hesitate? My house is well staffed. My housekeeper is the soul of rectitude and would stand for no untoward behavior in either myself or my guests. Rosalind, my dear, you are no longer in the schoolroom. Must you obtain permission from your aunt and uncle for such an innocent matter?" His eyes mocked her as he said, "Perhaps I am mistaken in you. I believed you to be a woman of spirit and not a namby-pamby, frightened creature who will never learn that persons of the *ton* need not worry about chattering tongues."

She was stung by his reference to her lack of experience in the social world; she raised her chin and said, "I should very much like to see your refurbished rooms, my lord."

No sooner had she stepped into the hall of the house in St. James Square than she realized it had been an act of folly. No one came to admit them, Sir Willton using his key for that purpose. It was late in the day and there was little light until he lit wall sconces which did not do much to relieve the gloom. No sounds came from other parts of the house and Rosalind, who had in that first moment felt a small thrill of fear, was now experiencing a surge of anger.

"Where is your housekeeper?" She shook off his hand which would have removed her coat from her shoulders. "Why is she not here?"

He pretended to look dismayed. "I have just remembered. She left this morning for Wimbledon to visit her sister who is sick there. I believe the maids, too, are taking advantage of her absence and on a holiday."

"The footmen also?" Rosalind's voice was hard, and there was fury in it. "You have managed to trick me, Turncroft, and it was the shabbiest of things! You have lied to me and put my good name in jeopardy and I am leaving this minute, hoping that I will not be seen by anyone as I leave this wretched place."

He threw back his head and laughed, and then, as she

moved toward the door, he placed himself in her path. His merriment suddenly vanished, and his face grew ugly. With an abrupt movement, he pulled her into his embrace, his mouth following hers as she turned her head from side to side to avoid his kisses.

There was such strength in his arms that she could not break out of the ring that they made around her body. He was breathing heavily, his chest heaving and his face red and damp. And for an instant, she thought that she was fainting as she lay almost helpless in his embrace. Then some inner power, perhaps her last ounce of strength, came to her aid for the briefest of moments, long enough for her to shove the man away by placing both hands against his chest and pushing. Her hands became claws which raked his face with her fingernails. He might have fought successfully against the pushing away; the scratches she inflicted upon him made him fumble, cursing loudly, for a handkerchief.

He did not stop her this time when she rushed toward the door. With her hand on the knob she cried over her shoulder, "My brother will call you out for this!"

She heard his ugly laughter. "A sprig, not over fifteen years old! You are dreaming, you teasing wench. Why did you think I wanted you here? To serve you tea?"

She did not look back at him. She did not need to see his face to know that she had made a powerful enemy this day, one who could ruin her with no more than a word or two.

Her first impulse was to run away from that wretched house as fast as possible, but there were people on the street and it was bad enough to be abroad alone at that hour of the day without calling attention to herself more than was necessary.

She prayed that she would meet no one she knew or any of Lady Mary's or Corinna's acquaintances, and she was lucky in that respect until she reached home. And then, breathing hard with the exertion of hurrying and with her hair loosened under her hat which was askew and her slippers damp because she had not tried to avoid muddy crossings, she found herself face to face with Sir Julian Wickstead, who was coming down the steps as she was ascending them.

7

Except for a flare of curiosity that appeared in his eyes, Sir Julian gave no sign that he thought it strange that she was returning home in the late afternoon without an escort, looking like the veriest dowd, disheveled in appearance, tongue-tied when he greeted her.

One of his most taking qualities, she had learned, was his kindness and as he removed his hat and bowed to her in the most civil manner, a great pain smote her; something of regret was in it, something of longing for what she would never have.

If Harriet had not fallen in love with him—if her sister's happiness had not been more important than her own—if she and the baronet could have met without the complication of schemes and plots . . .

There were too many *if*s, and for the first time she began to question the efficacy of her plot. She was wont to act in an impulsive and rash manner, not considering consequences. Just see what her foolhardiness had brought her this very day! She was not one to be easily frightened, but the results of her folly might affect them all.

Sir Willton, who might have the appearance, on the

surface, of a fop and a coxcomb, was someone who would not take calmly a rejection of his base desires. She was well aware that he would be ruthless in his revenge for what he would consider humiliation.

There was no one, of course, to whom she could confide her fears. Not to Aunt Mary or Uncle Charles, for they would naturally ring a peal over her head for having placed herself in such a situation. Nor to Harriet, whose timidity was such that she refused to leave the confines of her safe little world. As it was, Rosalind had the utmost trouble in persuading her, now and then, to join the strollers along Bond Street at the fashionable hour. It was for her sake that Rosalind insisted upon these outings. When the rosy plans came to fruition, Harriet would one day be the mistress of Sir Julian's estates and as such would entertain his friends and business associates with grace and poise.

Never once did Rosalind admit to herself that Harriet would not be the kind of wife that Wickstead needed. She was certain that once she had inspired love in his heart for this tall, slender girl who so lacked confidence in her attractions, all would be well.

Sir Julian was absent from the social scene for a few days and Rosalind ventured to ask Corinna his whereabouts. She made her voice as offhand as possible, as though this were merely a casual question, nothing more than idle chitchat. He had gone, Corinna informed her, to visit his lands and his tenants.

"He is most interested in the welfare of both," she said with a fond smile. "He has kept his inheritance in good order and is a credit to his name."

For a little while after that, life seemed dull to Rosalind. True, she had never been in Sir Julian's presence for more than short periods of time; but she found that she missed seeing his well-garbed figure striding into the drawing room for morning visits, his occasional presence at drums, balls, assemblies and the festivities at Covent Garden, all of which Lady Mary insisted her nieces attend.

Rosalind was both glad and sorry that there was no chance, at this time, of meeting the young baronet face to face at some unexpected moment. Until the memory of their encounter on the afternoon of that foolhardy visit to Sir Willton's house was erased by time from her mind, she would be uncomfortable. He had seen her at her worst yet he had tactfully ignored her ramshackle appearance on that occasion.

In the fine weather of those spring days, Harriet was willing to do as her sister suggested—spend more time out of doors. It took determined effort and bravery, for the mass of traffic frightened her with curricles, phaetons, barouches clogging the streets. Men and women in their best clothing strolled, stopped, carried on conversations. It was impossible to have walked briskly as both girls would have enjoyed more.

On one warm afternoon, when the park and Bond Street were even more crowded than usual, Harriet suddenly clutched Rosalind's arm.

"Look!" she gasped. "Up there on the box!"

She was pointing at a phaeton coming down the street with great speed, its driver weaving in and out through the traffic recklessly, missing by no more than inches a pair of young men on horseback who pulled out of his way swiftly.

The vehicle passed Rosalind so quickly that she had no more than a brief glimpse of the youth on the box. She turned to Harriet and they cried in chorus, "Freddy?"

In shocked accents they agreed that it had indeed been their brother. But what could he have been doing up there on the box, holding the ribbons in one hand and flicking the whip at the leader's ears with the other.

Rosalind spoke in a strained voice, knowing beforehand the answer to the question she was about to ask. "You saw, of course, who was with him, whose rig he was driving?"

"Yes, to be sure I did." The incredulous expression on her features was replaced by a troubled one. "It was Sir

Willton, was it not? The man Lady Mary has forbidden
us to accept as a friend?"

Her own feeling of guilt threw Rosalind into silence.
But it did not prevent her from seeking out her brother
later that day and giving him a rare scold.

"Our uncle and aunt would be up in the treetops were
I to tattle on you, you wicked boy. Sir Willton is no fit
companion for you, and this you must know. Too, you
were driving in a most reckless manner and have never
known the intricacies of driving . . ."

She had sought him out in the schoolroom, insisting
that Harriet be present, too, at the call-down. Matthew
Traynord was there also, looking most uncomfortable but
pleading no cause for his pupil.

"I am not a baby," Freddy said sullenly. "I think it the
finest of anything that Sir Willton invited me to drive
with him and let me take the ribbons. Those are a pair of
sweet goers, and he said that I will one day be a whipster
second to none."

"You might have killed yourself," she told him
severely. "Or the gentleman. You are not to have anything
more to do with him or his cattle, do you understand
that?"

Then she turned to Matthew. "May I ask how Freddy
persuaded you to allow him to embark on such a helter
skelter, care-for-nothing enterprise? Surely you must have
known that it would have been forbidden by Sir Charles
and Lady Mary had they had the slightest inkling of what
he was planning!"

Matthew paled and stepped back as though he had
been struck a physical blow. His Adam's apple bobbed up
and down as he tried to speak. But when he did it was
with dignity. "If you will not count it impertinent of me,
Miss Rosalind, I should like to point out that I am an
educationist and not a jailer. Master Freddy did not
consult with me before he went off with Sir Willton. Nor
did he ask my permission, which—if I may speak
frankly—he would have gone without at any rate."

That he was still overset was all too plain, and Harriet, seeing his distress, said gently, "Matthew is right, Rosalind. We all know that when Freddy makes up his mind to have something, no one can gainsay him."

She bestowed one of her sweet smiles on Matthew, and it seemed to perturb him even more. He did not even bring his glance back to Rosalind when she said, "You will keep a closer watch on him, won't you? It was not my wish to throw you into a miff, Matthew; I simply cannot allow Freddy to get into any scrapes, for the three of us are hanging upon Sir Charles's sleeve and what ungrateful wretches we should be if we should forget that that is so."

The young tutor could not remember ever having been so moved with pity. That this lovely girl, whom he worshipped from afar, was forced to toady to people of half her value kindled the fires of anguish in his narrow chest. Why, she was a pearl among swine, a star in a blackened sky, a gem in a heap of broken glass. His breathing sounded loud and uneven, and Harriet, believing that that condition was due to the set-down, met his eyes in a sympathetic glance.

Rosalind, unaware of the exchange of glances between the two, was plagued by a question that had been bothering her for days. A frown slid onto her forehead, she put a finger against her cheek in a familiar gesture of puzzlement and tilted her head.

"I swear I do not understand why Sir Willton must needs pay so much attention to us. Freddy, has he been seeking your friendship? Why did he invite you to drive his cattle? I, too—"

She broke off, blushing. She knew well enough the reason for his urging her to accompany him to his house in St. James Square. It had been for the attempt to seduce her. But even before that, he had paid her particular attention, not exactly courting her but unduly curious about Lady Mary, his distant relative, Sir Charles, who sometimes lost his amiable manner and had only a cold face to show to the young man, and the amount of wealth and possessions with which the family was endowed.

Since Rosalind and Harriet had scarcely a pence to call their own, it could not be thought that he was dangling for an advantageous marriage; indeed, had not Aunt Mary, who knew about such things, cleared him from the stigma of fortune hunter? What, then, had been his purpose in raining attention on Rosalind? Something besides passion, she was almost sure. Perhaps Freddy could supply the answer. But if Freddy knew it, he was obviously going to keep it a secret. For once he was close-mouthed.

"You must promise not to go out in his rig again. No good will come of it, you may be sure."

"The one person I have met," Freddy said rebelliously, "who knows what goes on in the world, and he cannot be a friend because of some silly fol-di-diddle!"

"We will say no more on this head for the nonce," she promised, "and I shall make no complaints to Uncle Charles or Aunt Mary about your conduct this time."

She turned then to Matthew and said in her usual impulsive way, "Pray, do forgive me! I was wrong to blame you, for I know what a trial Freddy can be."

It was Harriet only who noticed the young man's deepening flush and the moon-calf expression in his eyes. Poor Matthew; he, too, knew the pain of a useless and unacknowledged love! Her heart ached for him and she was determined that she, at least, would make certain to treat him with special gentleness.

Rosalind continued to insist that her sister accompany her in late afternoon strolls, pointing out that even though they did not consider themselves one with the ladies who walked out to display their finery and seize upon the opportunity to indulge in flirtations, the scene itself was amusing. There were gentlemen—Freddy had described them as being of a class known as top of the tulip—who arrayed themselves in brightly colored breeches and waistcoats with fobs and seals and intricately tied neckcloths whom the two girls counted as coxcombs. Ladies dressed in fashions not yet generally popular (hats of a military type, skirts slit to reveal silk-stockinged legs, bodices cut so low that generous expanses of flesh were exposed) were amusing to behold.

Now and then they would come upon a figure so totally out of place in that fashionable crowd that they would forget their good manners and turn to stare. There would be an old man who shuffled along, his back so bent that he seemed to be carrying a heavy burden upon it. Or they would pass a crone who muttered to herself, not seeming to know where she was or, perhaps, how she had wandered into this fashionable crowd.

Just such a one was the old lady who bumped into Harriet as she trudged along, her head down. She muttered something as she raised bright blue eyes to the girl's face and they saw that her face was clean, her features not unpleasing. Her clothing, too, though shabby, was not torn. Even her frayed shawl did not give her a look of hopeless poverty.

It was just at the moment of her passing them that Harriet looked up and saw only a few yards away from them Sir Julian mounted on a horse which he had drawn up beside a carriage bearing a crest. Beside the driver was a liveried footman. Its passenger was recognized by both girls at the same moment.

She was Lady Benedict, whose scandalous activities had kept London society in titillating *on dits* for several seasons, for Lord Benedict was a complaisant husband, his own flagrant affairs also material for lively gossip.

Her face was turned up to Wickstead's and a bold, provocative smile lay across her lips. Everything about her was inviting: the leisurely way she unfurled her long-handled sunshade, the bending of her body so that she could draw closer to him, the sweeping of her long eyelashes. She wore a velvet mantle and a Waterloo hat, the very latest in fashion, and her hands were covered by silk net gloves.

Rosalind, thrown into disorder by the sight of Sir Julian so engrossed in this boldly beautiful, notorious creature, took a step toward them without knowing that she was doing so. She moved off the path upon which she and Harriet had been walking, not looking in either direction and stepping blindly into the path of a curricle, the driver of which was engaged in a contest of speed with another vehicle only a few feet behind it.

Harriet, whose body seemed to be frozen in horror, tried to call out but her throat was clogged by a great, rocklike constriction. Nor would her hands and feet move, and for an instant it seemed that her sister must surely be trampled under the hooves of the galloping horses.

Then—and forever after to thank heaven for what must be a miracle—she saw the poorly dressed old woman they had passed only an instant before throw her thin little body in Rosalind's direction with surprising speed and agility, seize the girl, and push her to safety.

8

They fell together on the footpath, the old lady lying partly over the girl. For that reason and because her fright was of such debilitating effect that she could not have moved, Rosalind made no attempt to rise to her feet. Her heart beat hard and rapidly, and she could feel the trembling of nerves in every part of her body.

When she opened her eyes and looked up, she could see that a crowd had gathered for there was a ring of faces above her and those she recognized were Harriet's, pale and anguished, and Sir Julian Wickstead's, which spoke of his concern.

He reached down, put his hands under the old woman's armpits and hoisted her to her feet. When he attempted to do the same for Rosalind, she tried to move away from him. Instead, she put her hand into Harriet's and struggled to stand upright.

Her head began to throb where it had struck smartly against the ground. Tears of humiliation scalded her eyelids, for she was, she knew, a sad mess. Her chip straw hat had tumbled to one side so that its ribbon bow was not in front of her ear where it belonged but somewhere on the

top of her head. Without glancing at her skirt, she knew
that it was filthy and she made futile gestures to brush the
dirt from its French muslin and then tried to hide her
hands, all begrimed from her fall, behind her.

She wished that she could sink into oblivion, become
invisible to those whose curious glances were even yet fastened upon her as she tried to avoid Sir Julian's hand and
move away.

It was Harriet who held her there in a fast embrace.
"Oh, my dearest love!" she cried, much perturbed. "A
narrow escape you had to be sure! Are you wounded anywhere?"

"Only my pride. And it is not to be cured by standing
here to be stared at and pitied," Rosalind spoke miser-
ably. "Let us go home at once."

Sir Julian thought, not for the first time, what strange
creatures Sir Charles's nieces were: the one blushing
and unable to meet his gaze each time he was in her
presence, and the other of a nature as such to keep him
always puzzled. Enchanting as Rosalind might be with her
pretty ways, brilliantly expressive eyes and firm little chin,
a man would be gone in the noggin to let himself feel a
partiality for her—with this damsel, he would never
know where he was at!

And Sir Julian Wickstead had always known where he
was at with the ladies of his acquaintance. Of the
hundreds who had thrown out lures for him since he had
first come out onto the town, none had puzzled him.
Their motives were simple—they hoped to leg-shackle
him and lead him to the parson's mousetrap. What Corinna's cousin wanted of him he had not the slightest idea.
On the night of her come-out she had, for a brief space of
time, snubbed him. He had been amused rather than intrigued, for countless young beauties had tried all their
most devastating tricks upon him and failed to capture his
interest.

Then, during the few brief times he had been alone
with her, she had acted in a most hen-witted manner, fluttering her eyelids at him, smiling false and simpering

smiles, acting like a silly schoolroom miss in need of a call-down.

She had indeed captured his interest, but only the wrong kind, and he pitied Lady Mary, who must find an eligible husband for such a silly goose.

There were no smiles and eyelid-fluttering at this point, and her blushes came from her humiliation. "Come," he said gently. "I shall borrow Jeremy Arville's barouche and drive you both home. He lives not far from here, and the walk will not harm him at all. Here, over in this direction, he is the one with his mouth still at half-cock. For once he can be of use to someone."

It was Harriet who hung back. "It is too kind of you," she said, speaking for once in his presence in a forthright manner. "Rosalind's life was saved by this—this person."

She held firmly to the crone's arm. "No doubt, poor soul, she is hungry. We will take her home with us, and I shall see that she is fed. And perhaps we shall be able to find for her something to wear except those wretched . . ." She broke off, then said to the old woman, "It is not your fault that you are clad in those garments."

Harriet's tone was kindly, and her face was soft with pity. "Come along with us. There is nothing to fear."

Rosalind, her confusion clearing, felt now a twisting of dismay. If Sir Julian were to fall in love with Harriet, she should resemble the arrogant, poised Lady Benedict with whom he was evidently conducting a lively flirtation. Rosalind could not stretch her imagination far enough to visualize that notorious lady sitting beside a ragged crone in a borrowed carriage.

But there was nothing Rosalind could do, for Harriet was leading the old woman to the borrowed carriage, no trace of her shyness showing in her manner, seeming not to take notice of the bystanders and onlookers whom this small happening had attracted and thus lightened, for a very short time, the boredom of their lives. It was Rosalind who heard the titters and the whispers, and she wondered, somewhat fiercely, why Sir Julian could not recognize the worth of a determined young lady who cared only for the welfare of one of God's sad creatures and nothing at all for the opinion of idlers.

Rosalind, turning to the baronet, said in quelling accents, "It is most kind of you, sir, but we will . . ."

Neither he nor Harriet paid her any heed. He helped the two into the carriage, and she had naught to do but allow him to do the same for her. He seemed to have supreme confidence in his ability to guide a pair of strange horses, and he maneuvered his way through the crush of traffic with amazing skill.

Rosalind, her voice dropped low, inquired of her sister, "My dear, what in the world do you intend to do with this—this woman when we have reached home? Surely Aunt Mary will . . ."

She seemed destined not to put periods to her sentences, for once more she was interrupted. Harriet, shaking her head in a warning gesture, said, "We will talk of that later. Now we must think only of making this poor soul comfortable." She leaned closer to the woman beside her and asked, in a kindly fashion, "Tell us your name, do. What are you called?"

At first it seemed that no answer would be forthcoming. The surprisingly bright, light blue eyes darted from Sir Julian's back to Harriet's face and then rested upon Rosalind's chip straw bonnet which still hung askew over one ear. It seemed that she would not speak even a single word, but when they were only a few hundred yards from Grosvenor Square the pale old lips opened, and she pointed a bony finger at her chest and croaked, "Molly, me Molly."

"At last," Harriet said with a sigh of relief, "we know her name. So Aunt Mary will not look upon her as a total stranger."

But Aunt Mary, they discovered when the little procession filed into the drawing room where she was working with her embroidery frame, felt no such tepid emotion as dislike of someone she did not know entering her house. With the story of Rosalind's near brush with death, she promptly swooned into Sir Julian's arms, and for many minutes all was disorder, Biggers running for wet towels and smelling salts, Corinna rushing in to pat her mother's hands, loosen the woman's bodice and call to Haybolt the butler to summon a physician.

Lady Mary miraculously recovered at that moment. "It is a curse," she said weakly, "to be at the mercy of one's tender sensibilities."

She pulled herself up from the sofa upon which she had been placed, and her eyes fell upon the wispy little old woman who had been standing in one spot, regarding the scene with her bright, curious eyes.

Lady Mary's hand lifted and pointed. "Who has dared to bring this—this ragamuffin into my home? I have never, in all my entire life, had in my sight anybody . . . anything . . ."

She seemed to become bereft of words. Her face, mottled red, worked in a way that revealed her inner turmoil. As the woman named Molly, her old face lively with mischief, stepped closer to her ladyship, her chortling voice filled the room. "Then that places us even, ma'am, do it not? For never in me life have I seen the likes of you, neither."

For one awful minute it seemed that Lady Mary would once more succumb to a fainting spell. Her hand fluttered weakly upon her bosom, her eyes rolled back in her head, and she began to make mewling sounds of distress. Again her daughter, her dresser and her two nieces hurried to her aid; the towel was soaked in vinegar this time, her hands were patted more vigorously, and the smelling salts waved more rapidly under her nose.

Spectators but not participants were Sir Julian and the old woman who had caused the excitement. He stood, arms folded, regarding Molly, who finding his eyes upon her, gave him a wicked grin.

There was nothing about her that caused him disgust. He had seen her like many times in the city, hardy old creatures who managed to survive in spite of cold and hunger, beggars pleading for a pence or two. How, he wondered, would this situation resolve itself? And while he knew that it would, not be civil to remain there to witness the last act of this little drama, nothing could have torn him away. For the first time in many a day he found that he was not feeling the familiar boredom.

Lady Mary was seated upright now but still being ministered to by her dresser. Before she had a chance to speak, Harriet began a stuttering explanation of why she had brought Molly home. "So brave she was, dear aunt, so little regard she showed for her own safety! Surely she deserves a reward for saving Rosalind's life. Perhaps if, after she has been fed and given better clothing, she might be given work to do in the kitchen."

Haybolt, at that moment entering the room with a tray holding a pot of hot tea, cups and saucers and silverware, let it slide from his hands and stood in a state of shock, unable to give credence to what he had heard. When he recovered to some extent, he clapped his hands, but as a footman and a housemaid knelt to clean away the broken china and spilled liquid, his power of speech did not return.

Yes, Sir Julian told himself, it had turned out to be an amusing day. And he felt a little more in sympathy with Miss Harriet Bannestock who had never faced him without blushes and skittering glances, for he saw now that there was kindness under that awkwardness; and he hoped that Lady Mary would find for her elder niece an eligible *parti* who also would appreciate her fine qualities.

As for the other niece . . . Sir Julian grinned privately. He did not understand her strange behavior on certain occasions, and anything he did not understand interested him. Of one thing he was certain. Wherever Miss Rosalind was, there would indeed be something happening—something not always of an unremarkable nature.

Molly, because of the intervention of Sir Charles, went to work in the Bannestock kitchen. Sir Charles pointed out that Harriet had spoken the truth: They were indebted to the old woman for having saved Rosalind's life.

"My love," he said mildly, "there will always be something for her to do, some light chore. She will be an addition to the staff."

As, indeed, she was, but scarcely as he in his ignorance of what went on below stairs imagined. Mrs. Bastable, the cook, threatened to leave. Haybolt claimed that all work—and there was little enough of it—done by Molly had to be done over and thus caused labor of a double nature. The kitchen maids said bitterly that she was forever in their way, having not the slightest notion of how to go on when assigned the simplest of chores.

Only Freddy enjoyed her presence in the house. When he should have been busy with his studies, he was often to be found in some nook or corner of the servants' quarters engaged with her in earnest conversation. Discussing, Rosalind was sure, conditions among the poor, finding at last a listener for his theories on how to better their unhappy circumstances.

"But there is nothing we can do," she confided to her sister. "We simply cannot put her out on the streets. Sometimes I think Freddy may be right. Here we are, all of us, wasting great wealth on frippery things—fashionable dinners and clothing, the theater, Venetian breakfasts—all triviality when one considers the money might be better spent to relieve the misery of those unfortunates."

Harriet threw up her hands at the utterance of such heresy. She looked uneasily over her shoulder as though expecting to find someone who might have heard her sister's radical mouthings.

"You must not speak in such a way, dear love! Aunt Mary would find it most unbecoming. It is not for young ladies like us to concern ourselves with subjects like that. Oh, Roz dearest, if only you might find among our acquaintances someone for whom you could form an attachment! The weeks go by, and neither of us has yet had an offer."

"Indeed, you are wrong!" Rosalind said stoutly. "There were two, at least, who dangled after me, but I will marry no one who does not capture my heart."

That heart began to ache with a throbbing pain, as though it had been struck by a heavy object.

The man she loved, she was all too aware, would never be hers, for even before she had scarcely known him, she had assigned him to her sister, given her word that she would effect an advantageous marriage for the girl who could not do so herself. The man Harriet loved could never be anything to Rosalind.

It was on that very night when she had renounced all hopes and dreams of Sir Julian Wickstead that the first of a number of strange and disturbing happenings took place.

9

Rosalind awoke at some time in the darkest hours of the night, not knowing what had aroused her. In the bed beside her Harriet slept peacefully, her quiet breathing the only sound in the stillness.

But there had been another sound somewhere in the house, for why else would she have come awake at this time when not even from the street outside came the slightest noise? A strange feeling disturbed her; she could sense that something most peculiar was going on and while she was at most times a sensible girl without fanciful notions, uneasiness plucked at her nerves and drew her from her bed.

She thought that illness might have struck some member of the household, and with that fear uppermost in her mind, she put on a dressing gown and slippers and tiptoed to the door. At the other side of the hall, beyond the main staircase, was Freddy's bedroom. She was moving in that direction when she now heard an unmistakable sound— that of stealthy footsteps. Somewhere down there on the second floor, where were the chambers of Sir Charles,

Lady Mary and Corinna, there was an uneven flickering of a candle.

Rosalind went to the top of the staircase and leaned over. Down there in the long, dark hall only shadows met her eyes. Then there came into her vision a shadow that detached itself from the others and she saw the figure of a man moving into the meager light.

Her hand flew to her mouth but not in time to muffle the light scream which rose to her lips.

A pale blur of face lifted in her direction and even from that distance she felt the stab of the eyes of the man below her. She could see little else, for a hat brim was pulled far down onto his forehead. Nor, from that point, could she tell much about him: whether he was tall or short, of light complexion or dark.

She heard the sound of something striking against the floor, and suddenly he was gone, darting back into the shadows and disappearing somewhere down the main staircase. A door opened with a creak and shut with a cracking sound.

Rosalind moved slowly down the staircase and down the corridor until she came upon the object that the intruder had dropped and left behind. A guttering candle had been left on a marble-topped table, and she could see the outlines of a steel strong box at her feet. She was crouched down close to it when there was a sudden flare of stronger light and a rush of footsteps along the hall.

And then it seemed that all about her were all members of the household: Uncle Charles in a crimson brocade dressing gown; Aunt Mary, her face pale under her frilled and beribboned night cap; Corinna, looked as enchanting as though it had been midday in her lacy peignoir; Freddy rubbing sleepy eyes.

"What happened?"

"Who screamed?"

"What are you doing with that thing in your hands?"

The questions came rapidly, one after another, and although she tried to answer them all, her tongue became tangled and she could do no more than stutter words that made no sense.

"Silence, all of you!"

Sir Charles held up a peremptory hand. In his other he carried a candle which threw his face into hard planes of light and shadow. Rosalind had never before seen him with such sternness on his features. When the others were still, he spoke in severe accents.

"Now you may tell me," he commanded, staring at Rosalind, "why it is that I find you abroad in the middle of the night holding in your possession my steel safe box."

He took the object from her and tucked it under his arm. Then he waited for her to speak. She mumbled, "S-safe box? Indeed, I did not even know that it was that. I came upon a man, you see—well, not indeed to meet him face to face. But I could see him from up there," and she gestured toward the third floor staircase, "and when he saw me, he dropped the box and ran."

Sir Charles asked, on a quieter note, "You are aware, I believe, what it contains. Your aunt's and cousin's jewels. And of even greater value, the rose pin which has belonged, through the years, to the women of the Bannestock family."

He was gazing at her with great intensity while the others stood in a semicircle, silently waiting for the painful scene to come to a conclusion.

Now Freddy was there, too, and a step or so behind him his tutor. Haybolt stood a little way off, looking rather strange in his flannel bathrobe with his bare, thin legs exposed.

Rosalind saw them all like figures in a tableau, aware of them only as part of this dreadful nightmare.

Surely Uncle Charles could not believe that it had been she who had crept into his chamber and tried to steal the safe box! Yet he went on looking at her in that most peculiar fashion, almost as though he had never seen her before.

"A stranger," he said in a tone of doubt, "a burglar, although there is no explanation of how he was able to enter this house. Haybolt!" and he turned to his butler. "Am I to understand that a door or window was carelessly left open this night and so left us and all our possessions in danger? Might we all have been murdered in our beds by this intruder my niece claims she saw?"

Haybolt began to sputter denials. Arthur, the second footman, had as his duty the locking up of the house after all who lived in it were in their beds. Never, said Haybolt in a great bellow of emotion, had Arthur failed to make the house safe before. No, he claimed darkly, someone in the house had admitted the burglar. His suggestion was that the Bow Street Runners be summoned at once.

At that, Lady Mary clutched her husband's arm, seeming about to fall into the vapors. With a wave of his hand, he summoned Biggers who was fluttering about, her boudoir cap lumpy with the tightly rolled curls beneath it and her scrawny neck pitilessly exposed as it stretched above a limp garment.

They would not call the Bow Street Runners, Sir Charles decreed. Not, at least, until he had put a number of questions to certain members of the household.

Freddy, who had been quiet for too long, first demanded his say. "If you are thinking my sister guilty of stealing your gewgaws, sir, then you are all about in your head. She is not a thief, and I dare anyone to so imply. In that eventually I shall have to defend her name in the time-honored fashion. Traynord," he said, waving an arm in his tutor's direction, "will serve me as a second."

Matthew looked as though that would be the last thing in the world he would wish to do; and Rosalind, although touched by Freddy's championship of her, was nonetheless annoyed at his dramatic and meaningless gesture. No duels had been fought for a number of years, and even if they had not been forbidden by law, the idea of Freddy with a gun in his hand was ludicrous. Without doubt he would accomplish nothing more spectacular than shooting off one of his own toes. "Freddy!" she commanded. "Do not be a widgeon!"

Lady Mary's voice rang out suddenly. "That woman!"

she cried with her hand on her heart. "The one your nieces foisted upon us. She is the only stranger in our household. I make no doubt but that she opened the door tonight to one of her henchmen. Yes, that indeed is the answer to the mystery. Bannestock, you must send some-one down to her room and bring her here in order that you may confront her with her crime. She must not go un-punished!"

With a sigh which spoke of long suffering, Sir Charles dispatched one of the housemaids to Molly's small bed-room in the basement. Returning, the girl acquainted them with the fact that the woman was lying on her back and snoring loudly.

"And, by the sound and look of her, sir, I doubt she has been awake at any time this night."

It was plain that Biggers and the two parlormaids, along with a footman or two, were hugely enjoying this excitement, the like of which came only too seldom in this well-conducted household.

It was time, Sir Charles decided, to put a period to this postmidnight scene. "You," he said to Rosalind in a som-ber voice, "will join me in the book room. We must get to the bottom of this unhappy affair."

There was something quelling about the room, which he also used as an office, with its dark, paneled woodwork and its shelves full of heavy tomes which reached almost to the ceiling. The furniture, too, was of drab colors, and while it looked comfortable, it was not the sort of place which could be described as cozy.

Sir Charles sat down behind his desk and motioned to Rosalind to take the chair facing him. He cleared his throat once or twice, seeming to have trouble in beginning what he wanted to say. Because she could wait no longer, Rosalind blurted, "Dear Uncle Charles, surely you have no thought in your mind that it was I who took the safe box from your room with the intention of stealing it!"

He appeared to be a little discomposed by her frank opening of the subject. He removed from the pocket of his dressing gown a large-sized kerchief and swabbed his moist forehead. He stammered, "N-no, of course I have no notion that you are a thief. It is just that—that—"

She could have finished the sentence for him. He did not like upsetting happenings in his household. He wished that he might go on in his usual tranquil, even lethargic, manner, undisturbed by minor crises, arguments or any sort of unpleasantness.

". . . Carelessness," he muttered. "Not with deliberate intent to commit a crime, a window somewhere . . ."

"Uncle Charles," she said firmly, "you are not facing the issue. A robber came into this house tonight and tried to steal the jewelry that belonged to your mother. I saw him."

"Then describe him! That is the point of the matter, dear child. You speak vaguely of an intruder but you have told us nothing about him, not described his height, the shape of his body."

"Alas, I cannot!" She shook her head regretfully. "For I saw him only in the darkness, Uncle Charles. Please do not hold it against me that I cannot describe someone I saw only for an instant and then in the dimmest of lights."

"No, no." But he did not sound convinced. His thoughts seemed to be turned inward, and he sat looking at the point of the tent he had made of his fingers. "The thing is that the safe box contains the one piece of jewelry I should be most distressed to lose—the rose pin which has come down through the years to the Bannestock women."

He seemed to have difficulty speaking, and he did not permit his eyes to meet hers. "I am aware that you were disappointed in not having it come into your possession. Corinna apprised me of that fact on the night that I brought the jewelry home. Dear, generous girl, she felt it was unjust that you, who bore 'Rose' in your name was not its rightful owner." His face grew soft with fondness. "Who else could be so unselfish? I am convinced that there is no one . . ."

He broke off and his attention returned to the girl sitting silently opposite him. "Yes, well, there is no more to be said on that head. If it is true that you thought yourself entitled to this precious heirloom and succumbed to the temptation of pilfering it, I shall try to understand your impulse and we will say no more about the matter."

Rosalind said with a trace of bitterness in her voice, "Say no more about it! Let it stand that I am a thief, so dazzled by a little gewgaw which I never coveted? Corinna imparted the truth to you—I do feel that your presentation of it to her was unjust. But what should I have done with it had I taken it? What, indeed, would have been the purpose? I should not have been able to wear it; there is no place I could have hidden it from Harriet's eyes."

His face grew excessively troubled. "There are places where it may have been sold, the purchaser one of the unscrupulous scoundrels who pay little for valuable objects and then sell them on the Continent for exorbitant prices. Not that I am of a mind that you would engage in such a nefarious enterprise."

But for what other reason would he have questioned her along these lines? she asked herself. For a little while at least she had been under suspicion; and while now he was explaining in persuasive accents that the responsibility for keeping safe the exquisite little piece of jewelry hung heavily upon him, she could not banish the hurt which the matter had engendered in her sensibility.

Sir Charles patted her shoulder and told her to run along to bed. With his faculty to put the unpleasant behind him and easily regain his serene spirits, he was already putting the matter out of his mind.

Not so Rosalind, however. After the rest of the household members had returned to their beds and were presumably sleeping, she lay awake and wished that she had never seen nor heard of her grandmother's prized piece of jewelry.

10

But her wish was not to be granted. The subject arose, not many days later, in a most peculiar manner.

She had grown restless one warm afternoon, the confinement of the house too irksome to endure and decided to visit the circulating library which was not too far distant, in fact a comfortable walk for someone who enjoyed the outdoors.

Harriet was unable to accompany her because of the beginning of a sniffling cold. Biggers considered herself above serving her ladyship's nieces as an abigail, and if forced to do so would have shown her displeasure in a most disagreeable manner. The housemaids were all busy, the footmen were nowhere in sight; and so Rosalind slipped out of the house, her little excursion made more enjoyable because she was all too aware that Lady Mary would have forbidden it.

She encountered no one she knew on her way to the library, but she was halfway back to Grosvenor Square when a curricle pulled up beside her. She looked up from under her best bonnet (on that day she had gone forth in her most becoming day dress—French muslin with widely ruffled hem and puffed sleeves—and chip hat with ribbons to match) and for once she did not feel embarrassment about her appearance when she looked into the eyes of Sir Julian Wickstead.

Instead, a different sort of feeling smote her. Her heart began to race, her breath came with difficulty, her cheeks grew flushed as though from a burning fever.

She was in such a state that at first she did not notice that he was staring down at her with a lowering frown. He had removed his beaver hat, but she soon came aware that his gesture had been nothing more than an act of civility; it was all too plain that he found no pleasure in the meeting.

"May I ask," he said in a reproving voice, "why it is that I find you walking alone? Surely you must know that no genteelly bred young lady is guilty of such harum scarum behavior!"

"Oh, *poof!*" She was determined to brazen it out. "Do you think me so missish as to need someone always with me when I am not so very far from home? That, sir, bespeaks the restrictions of the schoolroom."

He jumped gracefully down from the driver's seat, put his hand under her elbow, and with no more effort than if she had been the lightest of burdens, he lifted her into the carriage.

"Not only may your name be ruined," he continued to scold her, "but actual harm may come to you. These are uneasy days in London; it can never be guessed when some malcontent may set upon one for the purpose of robbery and cause bodily harm. It is not safe for a young lady like you to wander about alone."

Again she sounded much disdainful. "I think you are doing it too brown, Sir Julian. Such gammon I have never before heard!"

"Nor should you even know the meaning of such vulgar language, let alone allow it to pass your lips." His tone had grown even more severe. "Only those who are established firmly in society and have enough consequence to allow them to be eccentric can speak in such a manner and not bring criticism down upon their heads."

She was cheered for no more than a minute by his concern for her behavior, allowing herself to be persuaded that he would not have given her such a scold if he were totally indifferent to her. In that moment she gave no thought to the fact that it did not matter at all what his feelings for her might be: He was causing her sister pain by scarcely acknowledging her existence, and Rosalind had resolved to change that situation.

Then Sir Julian spoke words which sent her sensitive heart plunging downward. "For the sake of your family—Miss Corinna in particular—you must be more circumspect. Your behavior reflects upon them, too; surely you must realize that. Their station is of the highest. It is to be supposed that Corinna will make a brilliant match . . ."

His voice drifted away, which might have signified, she thought, that he either was making plans to offer his hand to the lovely girl who was known as a diamond of the first water or had already proposed marriage and been refused. Rosalind's wayward heart gave a sudden leap when the latter consideration occurred to her. Then it settled down to the dullness of despair when she reflected that such a condition could never be. Who, she asked herself, would be so dimwitted as to scorn an offer from quite the most eligible bachelor in the whole of London?

As for him, perhaps he had embraced this opportunity to drive Rosalind home so that he might catch an additional glimpse, even a brief one, of his beloved. Silent as he was now, no doubt he was looking forward to that circumstance.

Sir Julian was thinking of no such thing. His mind was engaged with this intriguing child beside him with her strange contradictory nature; a child, indeed, one moment and the next with all the attractions of a grown-up lady. From the first he had been curious about her attitude toward him, but now, glancing at her sweet, girlish profile, he was even more so. What went on, he wondered, under those wayward curls? What was she planning in her silent thoughts?

When he turned the curricle into Grosvenor Square and the Bannestock house came into view, he pulled on the reins to slow down the horse's gait. Then he turned to the girl beside him and said, "Miss Rosalind, there is something I wish to ask you. I understand that your household was badly upset not more than a few nights ago. Someone, I have been told, attempted the thievery of a valuable piece of jewelry. Has not the guilty party yet been found?"

Rosalind became motionless, face turned straight ahead and only the clasping together of her hands in her lap betraying her agitation. She did not have to wonder from whence he had received the information of the aborted robbery. Corinna, of course, would have told him of it. They must needs be so close in spirit that there would be no secrets between them.

Or did he have another reason for his question?

There could be no reason. She was letting her imagination run mad. And so, when she recounted the story of the intruder, she did so in great detail and he listened intently, saying nothing until she had finished.

"And this was yours, was it not?" he asked when she fell silent. "An heirloom piece bequeathed to you by a grandmother? The loss, then, would have been yours alone?"

So Corinna had not told him the entire story, and Rosalind was determined that she would not. Nor would she say another word about the matter even though he seemed to be waiting, idling his horse, for her to go on. She said no word until he jumped down from the curricle and helped her out. Then she merely offered primly, "I thank you most kindly, sir, for your civility in driving me home."

He sketched a bow so deeply that he seemed to be mocking her. "I trust," he said, still on a light note, "I shall be seeing you this evening at the Todhunters' ball?

It is my hope that you will allow me to stand up with you for at least one of the dances."

A very short time ago she would have been thrown into the most pleasant state of excitement at words such as these; now the heirloom rose pin absorbed all her thoughts in a most disagreeable fashion. She wished with all her heart that she had never seen or heard of it, for nothing had gone as it should have since its coming into her life.

She was at the foot of the steps leading to the entrance door when she chanced to look up, her gaze pulled in that direction by a strong feeling that the eyes of someone were intent upon her.

A curtain on one of the windows on the first floor dropped hastily into place at that moment. Someone, she was sure, had been watching her as Sir Julian had been helping her to alight. It was just one more of the puzzling, disturbing occurrences which were plaguing her.

Once more Rosalind was awakened in the dead of night by a sound which broke the stillness. It was muffled, not anything at all like that which she had heard on the night of the attempted robbery. No matter, she told herself, pulling the bed covers up over her head. If there was noise as loud as the fireworks display at Vauxhall Gardens, she would pay it no heed, was determined to remain where she was and let someone else find out what was amiss this time.

But the sound went on and on, coming from the room exactly beneath her own—Corinna's boudoir, she came to realize. It was a most unhappy sound, unrestrained weeping, and fearing that her cousin might be suffering some sort of illness, Rosalind finally arose quietly and put on a dressing gown. Harriet, in her bed, stirred restlessly but went quickly back to sleep.

On a table in the hall, a candle was guttering, giving her little light but she had no trouble finding the staircase and then, on the floor below, the boudoir where Corinna wept in mournful tones into her pillow.

It was a charmingly furnished boudoir, dainty with frilled window hangings, satin wallpaper, delicate chairs and a generously mirrored dressing table. The curtains around the bed were of finest silk and the counterpane under which Corinna lay huddled was of a matching pale blue color.

Rosalind went directly to the bed and pulled aside its drapery. Corinna moved into a sitting position and the other girl, seeing her face in the moonlight that streamed into the room, was shocked by a face puffy from tears and blotched by a long session of crying.

Corinna turned back to her pillow. "Oh, do go away! I wish no one with me at this moment."

The peremptory dismissal in a harsh voice was so alien to the sweet-tempered girl that Rosalind was bereft of words. She reached out her hand and put it upon Corinna's forehead and felt it hot. She cried in alarm, "Dear cousin, you are burning up as though with the fever. You must let me call your mama or, not wishing that, you may be helped by one of the servants."

"No," the other girl insisted. "I want no one. For this is not a bodily ill which I am feeling and which can be cured by draughts and potions."

After a long, uneven sigh, she said, "It is a sickness of the heart, my dear." She was speaking in such faint tones that Rosalind could hear her only by leaning closer. "You do not know what it is like to love someone and lose him to—to—"

The harsh weeping resumed and brought Rosalind to her feet beside the bed. Astonishment shook her to the core of her being. She could not believe that the beautiful, much sought-after Miss Corinna Bannestock, one of London's reigning beauties, was feeling the anguish of despair because the man all had counted as her suitor did not return her regard. Sir Julian? Of course it must be he for although she might have suitors by the score with her background all it should be and the heiress to a fortune to boot, no other was in her company as frequently as the young baronet.

This, then, would be the reason why Corinna, having been out in society for three years, was still not betrothed. But surely she could not believe . . .

"Dear cousin, listen to me," Rosalind said firmly, "if it overset you this afternoon to have seen Sir Julian accompanying me home, it was no more than a civil act which he felt, I do not doubt, obliged to make since I am a member of your family and no more than he would have done for any female of his acquaintance whom he came upon walking alone. To be sure, he rang a peal over my head."

Whether or not Corinna heard her she could not tell. The sobbing was fainter now and the in-drawn gasps further apart. But she did not turn her face in the other girl's direction, and after a few minutes the weeping became even breathing and she seemed to have fallen asleep.

Rosalind went slowly and quietly back to her bedroom. The troubled thoughts engendered by the little scene in Corinna's boudoir would not be shaken off. Apart now from the unhappy girl, Rosalind could see things in a different light. She had jumped to the conclusion that her cousin was weeping over the fact that she and Sir Julian had been, for no longer than a quarter of an hour, alone together. What vanity that had been! As though she could prove any sort of rival for the affections of this man who could pick up any number of the handkerchiefs thrown at him. Perhaps it was Lady Benedict whom Corinna counted a rival.

It was indeed a tangle, Rosalind thought as she lay sleepless upon her bed. All three of them pining for the love of the same man: her cousin, her sister, herself. And perhaps even a fourth if Lady Benedict was not merely engaging in a light flirtation and had a real regard for the young baronet.

An ugly thought rose in Rosalind's mind. Little as she knew about the intrigues of affairs such as that between Lady Benedict and Sir Julian, she could guess that there were exchanges of costly gifts for favors received. Hearing about the heirloom pin, Lady Benedict might have coveted it and Sir Julian, so besotted with love, found someone among the servants perhaps . . .

She could not go on thinking along these lines, calling guilty a man whose lofty station and seemingly unassailable character she had admired from the outset of their acquaintanceship.

To count a man like Sir Julian a common thief, even though he might have sufficient means to have the actual crime committed by a paid flunky, was unthinkable.

What a scrape this was indeed! she thought in despair. There had been other lesser ones but never had her impulsive nature, so deplored by her papa, led her into making so many people unhappy.

For she blamed herself for Corinna's tears; if there had been no guilt in her mind, she could have stayed and comforted her cousin; if she had not encouraged Harriet to hope that Sir Julian could be made to see her attractions and come, in time, to fall in love with her—if, if, if . . . Everything she did seemed to have been wrong.

The decision to leave Sir Charles's house came slowly during the quiet hours of the night. Rather than remain there, where Harriet would go on meeting the man of her heart frequently and thus keep the wound of unacknowledged love unhealed, they would look for and find positions where they might be together—as educationists, perhaps, in a girls' school. Eventually the pain would wear away but tonight it was too sharp to be borne and Rosalind, too, had her spell of weeping in the unfriendly darkness.

11

In the morning she was late in arising. When the first few moments of lethargy passed away, her mind was caught up by thoughts as unhappy as those of the night before. Her plans were sketchy; lying ahead of her first was the talk she must have with Harriet. Then she must needs break the news to Uncle Charles that she intended to leave his house, make her apologies to Aunt Mary, bid them all good-bye.

At this point tears threatened again but she could not afford to waste time upon her own sad spirits; she must decide what to do about Freddy. If she appealed to her uncle to allow the boy to remain until she was able to take care of him, no doubt he would acquiesce.

While she was mulling over Freddy's future, there was a scratching at the door and Lizzie, one of the housemaids, entered the bedroom carrying a pot of chocolate on a tray. Engrossed as she was in her own concerns, Rosalind saw only vaguely that the little maid was wearing the strangest air. Her flushed, round-cheeked face bespoke of some sort of excitement and her voice climbed an octave and then fell back to its normal tones when she bade the other girl good morning.

It was not until Harriet reentered the bedroom, neatly clothed and looking wide-awake, that Rosalind realized that something was amiss. She learned of its nature immediately.

"She is gone!" Harriet said with a flutter of agitated hands. "At a time when the rest of us were sleeping, she must have slipped out of the house."

Rosalind repeated stupidly, "She?"

Her mind full of Corinna and her unhappy attachment, she found in her mind pictures of a carriage speeding over the road to Gretna Green, a hasty, scandalous wedding.

But of course it could not have been a more bumble-brained notion for Corinna Bannestock would never be guilty of such ramshackle behavior. And who then was Harriet speaking of, a veritable rattle as her words tumbled over each other? Then finally there was some coherence to her babbling.

"I thought she was happy here. I thought when we brought her home and settled her in the kitchen, she would feel herself valued and thus be happy. But no," and Harriet shook her head in great sadness. "She flew away like a little bird when its cage is opened."

"You are talking then of Molly!"

"Of course." Harriet put upon her a puzzled look. "Who else? She had few belongings, only what we bestowed upon her when she first arrived—an apron or two, new stockings, a comb and brush for her hair. She has left them all behind, which may mean one of two things: Either she intends to come back and reclaim them, or she wants nothing to do with us and the things we had given her."

There was still a touch of sadness in her manner and Rosalind could detect, too, a look of disappointment in her eyes. "Do not worry about her, dear sister, for we might, as you said, liken her to a bird who cannot be confined. You must not hope to change people like Molly, free spirits as it were. Nor can you hope to change the lot of the underclasses. Is it not enough that we have one member of the family inclined so? By the way, does Freddy know Molly has gone? If, in fact, she is? Might it not be that she left the house early this morning merely to take the air or for some other reason and will return at any minute?"

"I wish that it might be that way," Harriet said worriedly. "But it has been raining since shortly after midnight, I understand. No one, I judge, would be wandering about the streets unless for an excellent reason. I have sent Freddy out to walk a little way in the hope that he may come across her somewhere."

Freddy, Rosalind guessed, would be much disturbed by the abrupt departure of the old woman who, had the circumstances been different, could have been counted as his friend.

And so, for the present, Rosalind decided that she would not broach the subject of her leaving this house which had sheltered the three of them since the death of their father. It would serve no purpose since she remembered, belatedly, that Sir Charles had left earlier in the week to visit his mother's estate and finish up the odds and ends of business which needed to be taken care of there.

It was a long, disagreeable day of waiting: Rosalind for the sight of Molly returning; Freddy for his tutor to come back from a visit to his mother; Lady Mary for something entertaining and diverting to help alleviate her boredom.

Hardly to be counted as amusement was the visit of her dearest friend, Lucretia, Lady Fairlake who had come, she acknowledged with great honesty not because she craved Lady Mary's company, but because news had reached her about the Bannestock family heirloom, Corinna having worn it to an assembly at Almack's not many nights since, and she was eager to look upon it herself.

"Just another stroke of my poor luck," she mourned. "I was not present that night and must hear from others about something which my bosom bow has not seen fit to display to me."

Her round little face, not unlike Lady Mary's although they were not of a common kinship, was aggrieved and accusing.

"It was most unobliging of you, my dear, to have kept this piece of jewelry from my sight. But there! Life does go on sadly for some of us. We must bear our lot without complaint."

So saying, she began to list her complaints. "My abigail, who has been with me not under twenty years, is planning to marry our head groom. I could not believe such a shocking thing when it came to my ears. She is no less than eight-and-thirty and he of even more years. Certainly they are too old for such falldididdle, but they are planning to leave my employ and take up life in Brighton, where they will become proprietors of a rooming house there. With the money which I have paid them these many years. It is far from honest, and so I have told them!"

Lady Mary murmured sympathetic sounds, although her mind was elsewhere. When her friend began to embark on her other woes, a great list of them, she heard only little of them.

"And the Dowager Countess, Fairlake's mama, such a worry she is! When just this week, when I went to call upon her and make my respects, she sent down word by a servant that she was feeling indisposed and did not wish to leave her bed. Not to say that that is the worst of all. Soon Fairlake's relatives will descend upon us like a horde of locusts, for they favor spending the season in London and I shall be not much more than a servant, running at their beck and call, expected to find husbands for their two whey-faced daughters. Which, I fear, I shall never be able to do."

She let her voice die away and sat, hands in her lap, gazing upon her friend. "I must say, for someone who calls herself a person of sensibility," she said in a critical tone, "you show little interest in what I am enduring and will endure in the future."

Lady Mary expressed her apologies hastily. "It is not

disinterest on my part," she disclaimed. "But things are at sixes and sevens here on this day. See for yourself. No servants have brought up refreshments, for one of their number has disappeared; and although it did not seem that they held her in high esteem, they are worried and will not be easy until she returns."

Lady Fairlake threw up her hands in astonishment. "Can it be that you are concerned because one of your servants has flown the coop? Surely you must know, my dear Mary, that they are undependable to the point of hopelessness! Especially now that their leaders—odious men that they are!—are rallying them to protest against their lot in life. I would close my ears to their selfish demands but his lordship is most interested in politics, and the conversation when we are alone, or even with friends, seems to cling to this repellent subject."

Above all things, Lady Mary hated talk of this kind. She had no interest in knowing what went on outside her own well-conducted household, and certainly the subject, she felt, was not to be the concern of a woman of nobility. Yet today seemed not to be the time for conversation about trivial things, for even these two (called by their husbands rattles of the first water) found little silences falling between them. It was as though some dark cloud hovered over the Bannestock house.

"The pin," Lucretia reminded her friend at last. "You have promised to show it to me, have you not? Then bring it forth, for I have been most anxious to see it. Of course it is already the talk of the town and the envy of many."

Lady Mary was forced to confess that she could not be so obliging. "For Bannestock is out of town, finishing up—I most sincerely hope—the last of his mama's affairs. I do not have the key to the safe box, and so it cannot be opened until my lord returns. But then I promise you, you will feast your eyes upon it."

She let her voice drift away, uncertain as she was. She had revealed to no one—and had warned the servants of dismissal were they to spread gossip about the subject—

the story of the attempted theft. How Lucretia would
have loved that little tidbit! How greatly she would have
enjoyed being the center of attention when she was known
to be the purveyor of news—almost a firsthand partici-
pant in such a shocking happening—which could set the
town up by its ears.

So she decided to say nothing more about Molly's disappearance which was, after all, much ado about little. A
servant (and not one who would be greatly regretted if she
never returned) had disappeared, and it was thought that
she had done so through her own choice and so was not
to be worried about.

When Lady Fairlake took her departure, the day
settled down into dullness again. Because of the weather
there were no strolls down Bond Street or through the
park. The horses and rigs remained in the stable. The
young ladies were hard put to find something of a diverting nature to do.

And Freddy was more of a trial than usual. He interrupted his studies every half hour or so to run downstairs
to the kitchen and interrogate the servants, asking questions about Molly that he had already asked a half-dozen
times, thinking of new ones and demanding answers
which no one was able to give him.

His harassed tutor finally gave up trying to force his
lessons upon him. Poor Matthew! Rosalind thought,
seeing his rumpled hair, the worried look upon his face,
the deep color in his cheeks; attributing the last to the exertion of following his pupil upstairs and down. How annoying poor Matthew must find trying to teach a volatile
youth who had so little interest in learning!

He overtook his pupil in one of the smaller drawing
rooms, where Freddy was holding forth for the three
women who were all too plainly finding no enjoyment in
his prosing.

"Has no one any concern at all for an unfortunate old
woman who may already have been set upon by footpads
or murderers, whose safety no one cares a fig for? Is there
left in the world no such thing as compassion? I wonder

that you can sit quietly concerned with your silly little occupations while a human being roams the city, perhaps at the mercy of evil people!"

Lady Mary was affronted. Harriet was embarrassed and uncomfortable. Rosalind, understanding his distress, spoke out of sympathy and a desire to console. "Dear Freddy, you are going above everything! I make no doubt Molly has not fallen into the hands of criminals. Good God, for what reason would she be harmed? She would not have more than a few pence upon her person. No, she has simply taken a notion into her head to go off the way she came, with us knowing nothing about her. Perhaps she has a family somewhere about, friends, a life she never revealed to us. You must not excite yourself, Freddy, for you, too, will be a worry to us all, to Matthew most of all."

She smiled at the young man, whose face became redder. She had noticed before that Matthew sometimes acted in a strange manner when in her presence but never counted it more than his natural shyness. Now it came to her mind that he was not affected in such a manner by Aunt Mary or Harriet or even Corinna. But she put the thought quickly away, for Freddy was threatening to leave the house (a threat they had heard often that day) to go search for his friend.

"Say what you will!" he declaimed in strong accents. "She was my friend and thought on many heads as I do. You saw her as nothing more than someone to serve you, hands and feet to do your bidding. And do not pitch me that odious gammon about stations in life, for that did not matter."

He was, Rosalind saw, close to tears and she longed to put her arms around him and comfort him. But that would outrage him, she was sure; when he turned on his heel and fled from the room, she motioned to the others to let him go and make no attempt to follow him.

"He will be better off alone. I think," she said, turning to Matthew, "he is not in any mood for lessons today."

Lady Mary rose weakly to her feet and tottered in the

direction of the door. "My sensibilities cannot endure such scenes as this!" she said in a fading voice. "I must rest and try to recover my strength."

Harriet rushed to her side to give her support. "Dear aunt," she soothed, "you will feel better with a cold towel upon your forehead to ease the headache. Between Biggers and me we shall make you comfortable."

Rosalind, left alone with Matthew, picked up her embroidery intending to leave the room. But he strode across her path with surprising vigor, and when she looked up he was standing before her, a most puzzling expression upon his face.

"Miss Rosalind," he blurted, "it grieves me to see you overset by matters such as this. I wish I could lift from your shoulders all the troubles and worries that you must bear. I have felt so for—for these many weeks, but you are so far above me that I was constrained from speaking."

Too astonished to utter a single word, she stood with her mouth agape, staring up at him. He might have had trouble speaking feelings until this moment, but now there seemed to be nothing that could restrain the flow of words.

"Almost from the first moment my eyes fell upon you," he cried, "I knew that you would be the possessor of my heart forever! Oh, I am aware that your aunt has ambitions for you and lovely as you are, you will make the kind of eligible marriage that will please her!"

His voice had grown bitter and hopeless. His long fingers had lifted to his head and were raking his tousled hair. "You are far above my touch. I must needs always worship you from afar, like an earthbound creature gazing up at a star—"

"No, no!" Rosalind found her voice at last. Much distressed, she said, "You must not speak so, Matthew. You must not humble yourself. You are an educated man. You know a great many things most of us do not. Someday . . ."

She had been about to say that someday he would meet

a woman who would appreciate his good qualities and be proud to be his wife. But he misunderstood. Joyously he grasped her hands.

"I will wait forever! I do not care for how long! The sweetest word I have ever in my life heard was the 'some-day' which fell from your lips. Come!" He drew her closer to him. "Let us tell the others! I want the world to know that you are my promised wife!"

12

Certain that quiet, self-effacing Matthew had taken leave of his senses, she tried to slip her hands out of his grasp, but he clung to them, his face alight with a radiant glow. Rosalind was distressed that he had misunderstood her, and did not know how to tell him what she had been trying to say.

"Matthew," she gasped. "I did not mean that I would be your wife. I am deeply honored by your desire for my hand in marriage, and for that I thank you, but I regret that my feelings are such that I cannot accept your most obliging offer."

It was what Lady Mary had taught her to say if the offering party was hopelessly ineligible. Rosalind had never imagined that one day she would be saying the words to her brother's tutor. Nor was he accepting the refusal with the good grace and deep disappointment she had been led to believe would be forthcoming after such a rejection.

Deaf to her attempts to explain her refusal, Matthew was babbling on exactly as though her answer had been "Yes" instead of the opposite.

"Soon now I shall receive my post at one of the best

schools. We shall, of course, leave this house at the first possible moment. Oh, dear Rosalind—if I may call you such—we shall have the brightest of futures. Although our lot will be a modest one, we shall find love in a cottage not at all a lowering life, for with love to make the third member of our household . . . Until, of course, there will be a little stranger . . ."

He broke off, flushing, knowing that he had touched on a subject that was never to be spoken of between members of the opposite sex.

Rosalind seized the opportunity to make herself heard. The quelling words which were to have been uttered with sympathy and regret came from her mouth sounding as though she were giving him a ringing scold.

"Matthew, you are all about in your head! I thank you for the honor you have paid me, but I never shall bestow my hand upon you! Now let us say no more on the subject. I cannot think why you took it into your head that I should!"

"Dearest Rosalind, do not give me a refusing answer at this time. Perhaps I have been too abrupt, have frightened you with my impulsive nature."

Anyone less impulsive than Matthew she had never met. She made one last try. "I am honored by your proposal to make me your wife . . ."

He interrupted her with a snort. "I have no wish to hear such gammon. I shall wait patiently until you realize that we two shall deal exceedingly."

He fell to his knees and seized her hand. He was placing passionate kisses upon it and she was trying to draw it away when she came to realize that they were not alone in the room. As she turned she saw Sir Julian in the doorway regarding the scene with great interest.

Her faint, startled scream brought Matthew to his feet. "My darling, what bothers you. From now on, I shall protect you from all trials and tribulations . . ."

"You will protect me from nothing," Rosalind said, much overset. She was furiously angry—at Matthew, who had caused her the great embarrassment of being seen in the most ridiculous sort of situation, at Haybolt for admitting a visitor unannounced, at Sir Julian himself for the raising of his eyebrows and the one-sided twist of his lips.

She could have burst into tears had they not been held back by her stubbornness; she knew if Matthew saw the least trace of the misery displayed, he would embark once more on a lengthy prosing of the most melodramatic kind. The quiet man, once his emotions were released, would go on and on with his much disconcerting proposal of marriage.

No sooner had Sir Julian's footsteps died in the hall than Matthew said, "It is not at all easy for lovers to contrive to be alone. Come, now that we have the opportunity, let us seat ourselves on the divan and make our plans."

How was she to make him believe that there were to be no plans involving the two of them? What could she say that would convince him that she would never consent to be his wife? She refused the seat on the divan beside him and drew a deep breath to disabuse him of his notion that time would cast her into his waiting arms. Another visitor was on the threshold, this time announced by Haybolt. The last person in the world she wanted to see at that moment was Sir Willton Turncroft.

Matthew sprang instinctively to his feet. His flush was back in all its heat as Sir Willton raised his quizzing glass and examined from head to toe the man he considered not much more than an upper servant.

Rosalind, too, was wearing a flush which might easily be attributed to feelings of guilt. Her voice sounded as though it were caught somewhere in her throat, so embarrassed was she to have been surprised in this odious situation. Although she cared little for Sir Willton's opinion, she was outraged that, having spurned his advances, he now had found her practically in the arms of another man.

She managed to say icily, "We are not receiving visitors, if you please."

"So it would seem." He spoke easily, flicking an invisible speck of lint from his coat sleeve. "Matter of fact, it was not you I hoped to find at home. I came to call upon Miss Harriet, and so I have told Haybolt."

"M-miss Harriet!" She could scarcely stutter the words. Her brain was in a whirl. What, she asked herself, did this coxcomb wish with her sister? Only a short time ago, he had seemed to be paying court to Rosalind herself. Then he had managed to strike up a friendship with Freddy. And now here he was making a call upon Harriet, whom he had scarcely noticed until this very day. "I am afraid that you have wasted your time. I bid you good-bye, sir."

Still he did not leave. He lounged against the back of a chair, smiling his repellent smile. Much perturbed, she cried out, "My sister will not receive you."

"That I shall believe," he countered, "when she tells me so with her own lips."

Matthew stepped forward, his hands curling into fists at his side. He said, through clenched teeth, "Miss Rosalind has requested you to depart. I should advise you to do so without delay. Else," and he lifted the fists into a menacing position, "I must needs help you to do so. Your actions are those of a cur, and I intend to see that this lady's wishes are to be conformed with."

Sir Willton tossed back his head, and a great roar of laughter poured from his throat. Then he sobered, and his voice grew ugly. "Such talk is proof of your low station and vulgarity. Even the most ignorant of know-nothings does not speak so in front of a lady. So I will not engage in a fight with you now. But if you care to meet me in Jackson's saloon we shall see what you are made of; I am convinced that the first fiver I place on your face will put your brains ascramble."

"Stop! Stop!" Rosalind stepped between the two men. "Sir Willton is right, Matthew. This is not the place for such threats and quarreling. As for you," and she turned to the other man, "I find your presence most unwelcome. Have I not said so? Must I call a footman to force you to do as I command?"

He was about to reply when Harriet, her eyes big and

her face pale, entered the room. "Such a distressing noise!" she cried. "It is to be heard even as far away as upstairs." She looked from one to the other. "Matthew, what has happened? Why are you in such a state? Rosalind?"

"It is nothing to overset you, dear." Rosalind went to her and took an icy hand into her own. "It is simply that Matthew took exception to Sir Willton's calling at this hour. He is leaving now, and Matthew," she looked severely at Freddy's tutor, "has been delayed in going up to the schoolroom."

Sir Willton said silkily, "Your sister skirts the edge of the truth. It was you, my dear Miss Harriet, upon whom I had chosen to call. I and a group of friends are planning to attend the gala night at Vauxhall Gardens tomorrow evening. I have come to extend an invitation to you to join us."

Both girls seemed to have been struck dumb. Surely, Rosalind thought, much perturbed, she was not hearing what she seemed to be hearing. It was not until Sir Willton repeated his invitation that she came out of her dazed state.

"Will you then accompany us?"

Since Harriet seemed to be unable to answer for herself, her sister took it upon herself to do so. "That is not something Lady Mary could like," she said coldly. "I fear, sir, that you have wasted your time in coming here this day."

Sir Willton spoke in tones which almost matched hers in coolness. "Surely Miss Harriet can speak for herself. She is not a schoolroom miss, I believe, who must needs ask permission to seek pleasure in the company of a friend?"

His smile was odious, little more than a lifting of his lips. His gaze was firmly fastened upon Harriet's flushed face as he waited to see what effect his words were having upon her.

She answered him in a thin, far away voice. "I thank

you for your kind offer, sir, but my sister is right. I shall not be able to join your party."

Rosalind expected some sort of outburst from this man who must be used to being treated in a manner far different from that of the two girls who were regarding him with something far less than cordiality. He simply took his leave after civil good-byes, not seeming at all downcast, but, in fact, walking in a jaunty way as they stared after him.

How puzzling it all was! Rosalind thought uneasily. What could Sir Willton Turncroft possibly find entertaining in the company of the quieter, elder sister? First it had been Rosalind herself who had been the object of his attentions, then he had scraped up an acquaintance with Freddy. And now, for some reason she could not fathom, he had fastened his attention upon Harriet.

She found it a little frightening and wished there were someone with whom she could discuss the matter. But Corinna was distracted these days and so locked into some unhappiness of her own that it was doubtful if she could be of any help; Aunt Mary would succumb to the vapors if apprised of anything even slightly unpleasant; Matthew's emotions had become too volatile for him to be of any help; and Sir Charles was still absent on his business affairs, and no one seemed to know when he would return.

Things were to become even worse on the following day.

13

It started out as an ordinary day. There were a few morning callers, most of them friends of Lady Mary, a few Corinna's admirers. The weather was not of the best, rain was threatening and so Rosalind and her sister occupied themselves with indoor pursuits: the mending which always fell to the elder girl, writing letters to their few friends back in Sussex, glancing through the latest magazines depicting the smartest of fashions. The morning and part of the afternoon dragged slowly.

When Corinna came into the sewing chamber it was a welcome diversion. She was dressed in a riding costume of pearl gray with black velvet lapels, huge, matching buttons and white, ruffled neckcloth. Her hat was of black beaver with a scarlet feather along its brim; and she looked, as she always did when arrayed in even the simplest of dresses, breathtakingly beautiful.

But today she looked unhappy. Her eyes had lost their brilliance, her skin had no rosy hue, her lovely mouth drooped. Rosalind had seldom seen her cousin in such a mood as this, and she was astonished when Corinna invited her to ride with her in the park.

She hesitated because her own riding dress was sadly shabby compared to the one Freddy would have described as "all the kick." But it was plain that Corinna had a genuine need of her presence and so she said, "If you are sure that you want my company. I am not much of a horsewoman, being used to the slow, old cattle we had in Sussex. It seems, though, that people here do not ride for the sake of the diversion of riding but to see and be seen . . ."

Corinna was paying her no heed. Her eyes held that far away look which Rosalind had seen in them so often lately. She sighed, not looking forward to the outing but knowing that she must, since opportuned, provide company for the unhappy girl.

"If you will wait until I change my clothing, although I warn you again, dear Corinna, that I shall not be a credit to you, I will do as you wish."

Her riding costume, of heavy black velvet, was much too warm for a day of such damp mildness. Nor was her hat such that it could be described as of the latest fashion. It had lost much of its shape and its feather hung limply. But if Corinna noticed her cousin's shabbiness she gave no sign. She was silent, too, as they walked to the Bannestock stable to choose their horses.

Corinna's was a sleek, nervous chestnut, with a frightening way of tossing his head so that his silken mane danced and swung. For Rosalind, so obviously not a whipster, the groom brought out an older, less energetic bay. The girls were about to mount, when Haybolt, coatless and puffing from exertion, came running down from the house waving something in his hand.

Corinna went to take it from him. "Just arrived," he gasped. "Marked, you can see, 'Important' on the envelope."

She thanked him, her face suddenly becoming so radiant that a strong light might have been burning behind it. But when she looked down at the handwriting on the envelope, the light faded. With a lethargic motion of her hand, she tore the flap of the envelope open and took out a sheet of paper.

Her eyes had scarcely raced across the lines when her expression changed again. She thrust the letter into the pocket of her coat and with a single, graceful motion mounted her horse. With her hands grasping the reins, she swung him about and called to Rosalind, "Do forgive me! There is something I must do. Our ride must be postponed until another time!"

She was off then; the horse's hooves clattered on the cobblestones, becoming swifter as she touched her crop to its rump. For an instant Rosalind stood looking after her, bewildered, and then she, too, mounted, uncaring that many months had passed since she had ridden, distressed by that strange expression which had stamped itself upon her cousin's face—a look of great hope and anticipation. And a tightness which could be only determination.

Rosalind knew that it would be impossible to overtake her cousin, and yet she could not let her go off in this reckless manner, alone and riding through the streets of the city, where as she was vaguely aware, it was dangerous for a young woman to proceed unaccompanied. They were already approaching the part of London Rosalind knew only by hearsay, where crimes were committed practically every night and the teeming streets spelled menace. She did not look to see what was around her, for she kept her eyes ahead, trying to keep in sight the scarlet feather of Corinna's hat.

Rosalind lost it several times, but in the clogged byways progress was slow and at intervals, when the horse could do no more than inch along, Rosalind came within several hundred yards of the horsewoman she was trying to overtake.

Then she saw that they were leaving the city behind. There was a long stretch of open road with which she was unfamiliar. Not very far out into the country Corinna began to pull up on the reins and look from side to side as though searching for something or someplace.

She found it beyond a bend in the road, a shabby little

tavern with a sign hanging outside its door which read: "The Silver Crown." Its courtyard was muddy, there were a few underfed animals wandering about in front of it, no ostlers came out to take Corinna's horse when she stopped and slid down from the saddle.

No one greeted her, Rosalind saw, when she approached the scarred door, hesitated and then went in, her steps uncertain.

Rosalind sat for a moment, feeling her own uncertainty and such strong distaste that it was almost like illness. She could scarcely believe what she was seeing: the fastidious, genteelly bred Corinna Bannestock going into this dismal tavern to . . . to what? Carry out an assignation with someone who waited inside for her? There was not, in her thoughts, any other explanation.

Not knowing how she was to rescue her cousin from her folly, Rosalind drew her own horse into an empty space beside the tavern. A window on the first floor of the rude building was open, and she could hear voices coming from the room beyond. She had no trouble recognizing one of them as Corinna's.

". . . But you have lied to me, sir. You are planning not to live up to your promise." Sounding much agitated, she seemed to lose control of her voice which broke on a sob. "You find me helpless, sir, completely at your mercy!"

"Oh, come now!" It was Sir Willton Turncroft who spoke easily, almost insolently. "Let us not make a Cheltenham tragedy of it! I have told you the terms. You shall have what you want by merely giving me what I want. Fair enough?"

Rosalind slid from her horse, intending to join her cousin in the supper room and face the man who was causing the girl what was evidently deep unhappiness. But holding the reins in one hand and shading her face with her hat with the other, she hesitated in the side courtyard, not at all certain as to how she should find out what sort of scrape Corinna was in and what to do about it.

She acknowledged uneasily that her schemes to direct

the lives of others had not met with any sort of success. But she knew, too, that Corinna must be in some sort of mess and that she needed help.

It was difficult for Rosalind to surrender her fine dreams of capturing London's most eligible bachelor for her sister; and there was a little pain in her heart that had nothing to do with anyone else. Still, she must call upon him now for help in extricating Corinna from whatever difficulty she was having with Sir Willton.

Rosalind got back on her horse and turned him in the direction of the city. It was not until she had almost reached the fashionable section of London that it came into her mind that she did not even know where Sir Julian Wickstead had his residence. She searched her mind for a memory of any address she had heard anyone mention in connection with him. She could think of none. How aggravating it all was! she thought with dismay. Everything seemed to go wrong lately; it was as though some perverse fate were thwarting her at every turn.

It was past the fashionable hour for strolling and being seen in one's carriage. But she was lucky in her search for Sir Julian, for she saw him coming out of a building someone had once pointed out to her as being White's gambling club, walking in his easy, graceful manner, looking to be a man of great consequence, someone she would have noticed had she not even known him.

Drawing up beside him, she dismounted. It was not until he swept off his hat with a little bow that she realized she had no idea what to say to him. On her way back, she should have come upon something of an unalarming nature to apprise him of the fact that Corinna needed him and that he must go to her rescue.

"Why, Miss Rosalind!" He stood regarding her with twinkling eyes. There was something about this child that enchanted him; she seemed always to be up in the treetops about something. Bored as he was among people who were too often bored themselves, such liveliness intrigued him. "How," he asked, "may I serve you?" Indeed he knew that something was oversetting her for her eyes were full of pleading, her clothing looked as though it had received hard use and her face, which was beginning to seem more and more attractive to him, looked exhausted, as though she had ridden too far too fast.

Her mouth opened and then closed again. It had seemed so simple just a short time ago, she need only find Sir Julian, enlist his aid, and all the difficulty would disappear. But it was not as easy as she had thought. How did you tell a gentleman that the woman he loved was in the presence of another gentleman in a ramshackle tavern and engaged with him in a strange sort of conversation. No doubt Sir Julian put Corinna on a pedestal and no matter what it was that had embroiled Corinna and Sir Willton in a shoddy situation, he might take it into his head that she was not the blameless goddess he believed her to be.

"Oh, Sir Julian!"

Rosalind's hands clasped each other and her face became even more distressed. "You must—you must do something!"

"To be sure, I will," he said cordially. "You have only to tell me what it is you wish me to do."

"That is it. I cannot—I cannot. Well, to be sure I can say what must be done but not the reason. Do you understand me?" She peered anxiously up at him. "Will you favor me with your help?"

"To be sure," he returned, "unless it is something so grave it might mean the loss of my life. But there! Perhaps I should not quibble over trifles. Yes, Miss Rosalind, I shall do all in my power to assist you in any way I am able, even though it mean receiving a bullet in my chest or a sword between my ribs."

Peering up at him, she could see the twitching of his lips. She cried sharply, "It is a most serious matter, I assure you, sir. There is—there is a certain lady who is in the worst possible scrape. It seems she went to meet this gentleman—no, I shall not call him thus! They met, and it seems he had made a promise to her which he did not keep and she is most angry as who can blame her? But I believe she might be in danger, for he is a most unsavory character and one with whom no respectable young lady would cry friends, as well I know since on one occasion which I wish not to speak about now, I, too, was—was at much disadvantage. With this same man although not in a tavern beyond the city."

She realized that she was saying too much but was relieved to learn that he seemed more confused than skeptical about her outpouring. He stood biting his lip for a moment and then said, "Why do you not tell me the whole story?"

Her heart sank. She had no choice now but to do as he requested. Omitting the part about her own disagreeable encounter with Sir Willton Turncroft, she told him how Haybolt had delivered the letter to Corinna, her ride through the city, following her, and—as a climax to the whole mysterious affair—the conversation she had heard between the two in the supper room of the Silver Crown.

During her narration Sir Julian's face had been changing color and was now a dark, angry red. But when he spoke, his voice was quiet, and it took her a few minutes to realize that it was an ominous quietness.

"You must not bother yourself about this any longer, my child," he said. "You can leave it to me to take care of everything."

He seemed to be about to say more but bit off the words; and it was then that Rosalind began to feel frightened. Would the two men on some deserted field in the pale light of dawn, engage in a duel—something she had heard about in her childhood? Had she, by revealing the rendezvous of Corinna and Sir Willton, sentenced a man to death?

"I will escort you home," Sir Julian said, still in that grim voice, "and you may forget what you have heard and seen. I think it best that you forget what has happened this day. Yes," he added sternly, "it will serve nothing for you to dwell upon it nor to reveal to anyone else what you have told me. Understood?"

She could do no more than nod. Once more, she thought with great regret, she had acted rashly, given in to her impulses without thought for consequences. This time, however, her lack of foresight might be serious. With only the best of intentions, she might have caused the death of one man and made a murderer of another.

Things appeared a little brighter that evening, for Sir Charles Bannestock, his business finished, returned home.

14

He found his household in sad disorder. His wife had a dozen complaints. The Tramworths had not sent them an invitation to their Venetian breakfast. Her new purple satin gown, returned only that day from the mantua maker, did not fit as it should. His two nieces did not receive as many callers as they should, and she was sorely afraid that she would never find them eligible husbands. Freddy had been insolent to her and—oh, yes, the old woman—Molly, whom she had sheltered out of the kindness of her heart (Lady Mary had the most convenient of memories), had simply walked away without saying a word about her intentions.

"You are overset because a servant left our employ?" Sir Charles asked incredulously. "And one whom you misliked from the start? How many times have I heard you say it was beyond Christian charity to allow her to remain in our household?" His forehead wrinkled. "Does my memory serve me right when I recall that the other servants felt put upon because they did so much more work than did she? And did I not hear that you scolded Freddy for having spent time in the kitchen engaged in conversation with her? Why, my love, do you look upon her leaving as some sort of crisis when I should expect that you would be relieved to have her gone?"

Lady Mary had no answer. Her fat little hands waved vaguely. "I never favored her working here. But she disappeared so strangely . . ."

"Let us talk no more about that. I cannot like returning home after being away to find that trivial things have become so important."

They were gathered in the yellow drawing room, and it had seemed, for a little while that evening, that the reunion between the master of the house and his family was to be a pleasant occasion.

But when the subject of Molly came up, Freddy began to glower. His lower lip was thrust out, and his eyes burned with an angry light.

"You all speak as though she matters not at all, except as an inconvenience. She is a person, and she is out there on the streets somewhere, hungry perhaps, or at the mercy of footpads and thieves and murderers. I have wanted to go and search for her, but no! Most important of all are my lessons—dry stuff learned from books. My good tutor insists that I miss not a one, tyrant that he is."

Matthew was not there in that family gathering, for which Rosalind had at first been much relieved. A face-to-face meeting would have been awkward and perhaps even embarrassing after the scene in the other salon, when he had poured out his romantic declaration.

But on the other hand, Matthew had always acted as a buffer between Freddy and his guardians. Without the restraining hand of his tutor, Freddy began to declaim upon the misfortunes of people like Molly and the injustice of class systems.

"That," Sir Charles said sternly, "will be enough of that sort of talk from you, young man. When you are old enough to know something about the subject of which you speak, we will listen to you. In the meantime, I will appreciate your silence."

His glance turned to Corinna and softened. "How is it,

my dear daughter, I find you in such poor spirits? When I left you were blooming and happy. Now I must confess I see you—well, almost haggard. What has happened to put you into such a state?"

Lady Mary put in: "Such a whirl as she has been in, Bannestock! Again this season she is the reigning belle of London. I declare, she must have had a dozen offers, one from an earl, but she refuses them all and clings to the notion that she must marry only for love."

Rosalind expected that he would smile fondly at his daughter as was his wont and call her a "silly puss," but he did not lose his sober expression.

"We must always keep in mind the danger of allowing strangers into our household. There are things of great value here which might tempt one of the poorer classes. Speaking of which," he addressed Corinna, "I hope you have enjoyed wearing Mama's rose pin; did you not do so? Were you not the envy of those who saw it upon you?"

Again this time it was Lady Mary who responded. "It has been seen upon her only seldom. She has not taken a liking to it, although she might have been expected to do so. Besides, my love, only you have the key to the jewel case," she reminded him. "We have been sorely without ornamentation during your absence."

She tittered to assure him that she was speaking in jest, but that, too, left him with a sober mien. "Dear daughter, were you not wearing it on the night I left? Going out to a ball, I believe, with the most insistent of your suitors— Sir Julian? I was not here when you returned and so have no way of knowing whether or not you placed it back under lock and key. Most worrisome, I vow. Especially since there was someone none of us knew here under our roof, who, you say, has taken herself off with no explanation."

Freddy cried hotly, "Molly was not a thief, and so I shall say for times without number. Besides you are accusing her when you do not even know whether or not your bauble is not exactly where it belongs!"

"There," his uncle said, in a more soothing manner this time, "I have accused no one. But just to make certain I shall go upstairs and see. If you will all wait here for me, I shall be back in a very few minutes."

Much more time than that passed before he returned. The others in that cold, lemon colored room were growing uneasy until they heard, at last, the sound of his approaching footsteps. One glance at his face told them the truth.

He confirmed it by saying: "The rose pin is gone!"

The search began the very minute after he announced that although the box containing the little pin had been locked, when he opened it there was no bejeweled rose with the other ornaments.

The others were stunned. Only Lady Mary spoke. "But, my love, how was it taken then—if such it was? You have the key and the key was needed for someone to unlock it."

He nodded in cold silence, then ordered them all to begin to turn everything in the house upside down. He would himself, he announced, question the servants: all of them, from Haybolt and Cook down to the lowliest scullery maid and footman.

Freddy, hopping about beside him, kept up a steady stream of chatter, most of it designed to defend the old woman who, he declared, was not a magician and could never have spirited something out of a locked box.

His uncle bade him to be quiet and join the others in ransacking the house in quest of the pin which, he pointed out, could not have walked away by itself.

The questioning went on until late in the evening, with various reactions of those who as one man denied any complicity in the theft. Haybolt was grievously insulted; Cook threatened to leave; Lizzie, the youngest housemaid, burst into tears and could not be consoled.

"Treating us," she sniffled, "like we was criminals. I never seed their ruddy old pin, for that matter, and so I shall go on saying until the day of my last prayers!"

Supper was extremely late that night, a silent, mournful meal for those who served it and those who ate little of it. Before it was cleared from the table, Sir Julian arrived to take Corinna to a rout party about which she candidly informed him she had forgotten. After hearing about it Sir Julian suggested that their crisis be reported to Bow Street, but both Sir Charles and his lady promptly and definitely refused to consider the idea. Perhaps in the morning, they temporized. The search would be resumed after supper. If the pin had not been discovered by then . . .

"And they will track down Molly," Freddy said with great bitterness. "It will be easy for them to find her, and she will be guilty in their eyes, as she is in yours, and no doubt thrown into jail to spend the rest of her life there."

Sir Charles, made testy by worry and distress, bade him once more to be silent. "You speak of things you know nothing about," he said severely. "If this Molly, whom I have yet to set eyes upon, is guilty, then she must, indeed, appear before a magistrate. It would help matters if we could give the Runners a description of her. My love," and he turned to his wife, "can you tell us anything about her appearance?"

Lady Mary seemed anguished at the thought of using her brain for any reason. "I do not think I can remember. The others . . . perhaps the others . . ."

"She saved my life," Rosalind said quietly. "And yet I cannot recall her face except that she was wrinkled, but had a smile that seemed quite warm and friendly." She turned to her sister. "Did you remark anything particular about her?"

No one, it seemed, had done so except Freddy and no one seemed willing to listen to him. Sir Charles proposed a sort of compromise: he would wait until the morning before reporting the theft to the Bow Street Runners, and if the valuable piece of jewelry was not returned by then, Molly must take her just punishment if she were found.

But in the morning, Freddy, too, had disappeared.

15

They were sitting glumly at breakfast when Matthew Traynord came rushing into the room. It was not at all like Freddy's tutor to seek out any member of the family unless he made a formal request; usually he waited until he was summoned to the master's presence. Because of his shyness, he found a conference, brief as it might be, much perturbing, for he was much in awe of Sir Charles.

To have him burst into the dining room while the family was gathered there at table was so little like his usual demeanor that all of them—the three young ladies, Sir Charles and his lady—looked up in astonishment and stared at the young man whose hair was tousled and whose eyes held a wild sort of look.

"May I ask," Sir Charles began, "how it happens that . . ."

Matthew interrupted him, something which none of them had ever dreamed would come about. "You have my apologies, sir, but I could not wait for Haybolt to summon you. It is Freddy, you see, and I knew that you must be apprised at once."

There was not exactly a sigh which rose in chorus

around the table. It was merely a deep breath, possibly in some cases of relief, for all of them knew that Freddy was harassing his tutor with some sort of mischief, no doubt. His fits of defiance, as sometimes happened, seemed no more than natural.

Then Matthew blurted, "He is gone!"

"Gone? Gone where?" It was Sir Charles who asked the question and the others, their attention captured, waited for the answer.

Matthew drew a deep breath. "That is it, sir. When he did not appear for his lessons at the usual time, I left the schoolroom where I had been waiting and went in search of him."

The word "search" seemed to hang in the air. There had been, quite too many searches in the past two days: for Molly, for the rose pin, and now here was Matthew talking about searching for Freddy.

Harriet jumped to her feet; quiet, self-effacing Harriet who seldom spoke unless she was addressed, who would never find herself shaking a man's sleeve as she was doing now unless she were agitated beyond any control.

Pulling at Matthew's arm, she cried. "Surely you must have overlooked someplace. Perhaps he is out on the streets somewhere. You know what Freddy is like, Matthew. He believes himself to be the savior of the downtrodden and unfortunate. I make no doubt he is even now on a street corner somewhere or in the park listening to someone haranguing. Can you not see him at this minute. . . ?"

"No," Matthew told her quietly, gently putting his hand over hers. "For there are no orators about during the night. And Freddy, you see, left when we must all have been sleeping. For his bed was not in the least disturbed and had not, I fear, been lain upon. The counterpane and pillows were as the girls had arranged them. And I have asked them—the servants, I mean—if this was not so. There does not seem to be," Matthew said, sounding reluctant, "any of his clothing missing."

"I will take a look." Sir Charles rose to his feet. "There

must be some explanation for this turn of affairs. People do not simply vanish into the air. This will be one of his tricks, perhaps to get his own way in some manner." He looked around the table with an expression upon his florid face which was intended to be reassuring but which was not. "Pulling a caper," he said more loudly, but he did not manage to convince anyone.

Rosalind and Harriet, knowing Freddy better than the others, were aware of the penchant for mischief which had made his childhood years a trial. Then, suddenly, he had grown up and at fourteen he had developed ideas not at all in keeping with his station, much to the discomfort of his family. Somehow, since Freddy and his sisters had been living in Sir Charles's house, Matthew had managed to restrain his pupil from giving outright offense, but now he began to speak his mind and what he said brought no comfort to those assembled in the dining room.

"He was much agitated by the disappearance of the woman we knew as Molly. I believe that they became," and he looked apologetically at Lady Mary, "what one might call good friends. Many times, when I sought him out because he was neglecting his lessons, I would find him down in the kitchen, engaged in conversation with her. I never heard much of what they were saying, but from a word here and there I gathered they were discussing—well, social conditions. I might say, if I may be forgiven, that he seemed quite fond of the old woman."

"But how could that be so?" Lady Mary cried, much bewildered. "She was but a servant!"

So overset was she that it was necessary for Biggers to be called and smelling salts to be waved under her ladyship's nose. She lay back in her chair, moaning lightly, until Sir Charles said grimly, "If the young sprig plans to frighten us into acceding to some wild demand of his, he will find himself much disappointed. It is my belief that he has staged this little drama to call attention to himself or because he is angry that we are not more concerned about his newfound friend. So we should remain calm in the face of what we are supposed to consider a frightening circumstance. You ladies," and he looked at each of them in turn, "will proceed with your affairs as though nothing has happened. As for you," looking at Matthew, "you will cudgel your brain to think of anywhere he might have gone, anyone who might give him shelter. I am not sure, Traynord, that you are the best of tutors for my nephew. One of your duties, as you must know, is to make sure that he feels about things as he should. Under your tutelage, he has almost turned into a revolutionary . . ."

"Oh, Uncle Charles!"

It was Harriet who cried out. Her face was highly flushed and her eyes, usually serene and gentle, seemed to be shooting sparks.

"How unfair you are, my lord! It is not at all Matthew's fault that Freddy has these idiotish ideas. I have myself heard him arguing with that wretched boy!"

She stopped, sent one distressed glance at Matthew and then was about to flee from the room when Rosalind grasped her arm and drew her close to her side. "Sister is right. We should not blame Matthew for this miserable affair. I think we should all be concerned about only one thing—finding Freddy. As for the pin . . ."

For an instant she could not go on. Then she said, with something of her old spirit, "I refuse to believe that the theft of the pin has anything to do with Molly's disappearance. Or Freddy's. Neither of them would know what to do with it as I should not have had Uncle Charles not so informed me."

No one seeming to have any desire to eat, the breakfast table was abandoned. Lady Mary managed to gasp to Haybolt, who fluttered about much interested in what was taking place, that no visitors would be received. "For I fear that I must lay upon my bed while my nerves are in poor shape. Come, Biggers, and assist me to my chamber."

There was, however, one caller that morning. Sir Julian Wickstead, impeccably dressed in a riding coat of many capes, spotless fawn pantaloons and Hessian boots as shiny as mirrors, would not be denied entrance. Forcing Haybolt aside with a wave of his long hand, he strode into the downstairs drawing room where the three young ladies of the household were trying without much success to occupy themselves with embroidery. His appearance caused a flurry, for none of the three had found the heart to bother at great length with her toilette and were wearing morning dresses which were not their best.

Of the three Corinna looked her usual enchanting self, but Rosalind and Harriet were pale with worry and were merely dismayed in the presence of London's most handsome and sought-after bachelor.

He felt the strained atmosphere and demanded to know what was oversetting them. Why not tell him? Rosalind thought, attempting to maintain an air of indifference. He would undoubtedly soon be a member of the family and although she received from Corinna a negating frown, she saw no harm in confiding to Sir Julian the strange, unexplainable things which had been happening.

He was silent while she was speaking. Never before had he seen her in this mood; usually she seemed to be facing up to life with a stubborn sort of courage. Now, speaking of her brother, there was under her valiant effort to be calm a fear which she could not quite hide. It looked out of her beautiful eyes and was evident in the occasional trembling of her lips. He had a strong impulse to take her into his arms and comfort her, but of course that was out of the question. She had intrigued him from the very beginning, but her actions when heretofore he had been in her presence, he had not been able to understand since she was one minute cordial and the next coldly quelling.

Too, a very long time ago he had made a tentative offer for Corinna's hand. They understood each other perfectly. He had said, "If, by any chance you do not marry the one you really want . . . I think we might deal exceedingly since neither of us would expect too much from the other."

And she had replied, "Dear Julian, you are the kindest

of men! It would not be to my liking to make of you second-best. You deserve much, much more: someone who will adore you."

They were talking the situation over when Matthew, looking much bedeviled, came as far as the threshold and then checked, ill-at-ease as he usually was when he found himself in the presence of the young baronet. Poor Matthew! Rosalind thought, but not pitying him for the usual reason. Freddy was not present to make his life miserable, but no doubt he held himself responsible for the disappearance of his charge.

He had come to report that one of the grooms from next door believed he had seen Freddy some time after midnight, when he had remarked upon it because it had seemed much too late for a youth of his age to be abroad. The information was useless, as it was impossible to find anyone who had been seen some sixteen hours before. Nor were the other clues as to Freddy's whereabouts of any value. When the news of his disappearance spread from house to house by way of the servants' grapevine, there were other claimants to information about him, some who genuinely believed they had news of him, others hoping for rewards for their trumped-up stories.

The long day came to an end, and still there was no trace of Freddy. Rosalind and Harriet had spells of weeping; Lady Mary was under the care of Biggers; Corinna wandered about the house like a restless ghost. Sir Julian remained, and an extra place was set for him at dinner time. Rosalind had never seen this part of his nature: the kindliness and concern for others, his gentleness toward all of them as darkness began to fall. He seemed to sense that these would be their bad hours, especially for Freddy's sisters, who were imagining him out in a strange city meeting all sorts of peril.

Just at the moment the candles inside the house and the flambeaux outside were being lit, the letter arrived.

16

The door knocker had made its raucous sound, Haybolt had come upstairs to answer it, the letter had been
thrust into his hand. That was all Haybolt could tell them
when Sir Charles had summoned everyone to join them
in the yellow drawing room.

He had not had a good look at the man, Haybolt insisted. It was not exactly dark on the door stoop, but the
torches threw only an uneven light on the messenger's
face. All he could say was that the creature had been
rough looking, not a gentleman by any means; not, he
sniffed, the kind of person he was accustomed to admitting to the house.

Haybolt would have lingered, for his curiosity was at
that moment stronger than his dignity, but Sir Charles dismissed him and he left slowly and unwillingly.

Then Sir Charles, slapping the piece of paper against
his palm, told them what it contained. He had read it
through hastily, and he was much perturbed as he
perused it again. In a hoarse voice he began to read it
aloud.

"You will understand," he said after reading one sentence, "that this is most crudely written. Words are misspelled and it appears to be the work of an unlettered person. Well, I shall start again and you are to listen carefully.

" 'Sir,' " he began again, " 'if you wish to see your nephew alive you will have to pay for his return. We have him as a prisoner and will hold him until we receive a goodly sum from you. It will cost you ten thousand pounds to get him free and before long you will receive instructions.' "

"That is all?" Rosalind breathed. "Oh, dear sir, I feel as though we are all living in a nightmare. Poor Freddy! To threaten his life in this manner! Surely he will not be harmed! Whoever wrote that wretched note merely wishes for money, is not that so?"

Sir Charles seemed not to wish to meet her eyes. His face wore a bleak expression as he turned the piece of paper over and over again in his hands. He tried to speak reassuringly but failed.

"To be sure this is but an idle threat. I doubt that Freddy was abducted . . ."

"But we cannot take that risk," Corinna put in quietly. "Poor child! He is scarcely more than that, you know. You must pay these dreadful criminals the money they ask for. Do you not agree?"

She glanced around the room: at her two cousins, whose eyes were full of fear for the safety of their brother; at Matthew, with his suffering, hangdog look; at Lady Mary, who was moaning softly under her breath; and, finally, again at Sir Charles, who was acting very strangely indeed.

He was shredding the edges of the letter, which should have gone to the Bow Street Runners immediately. His forehead was puckered in a way that looked more anguished than worried. With his hands behind his back, he began to pace the length of the room. When he spoke once more, it was to Matthew.

"I must ask you to leave us for a few minutes, Traynord." Sir Charles, who had at times treated those below his station in a high-handed and even overbearing manner, sounded almost humble. "There is some family business to be discussed. And Sir Julian, I pray you will excuse us."

Sir Julian excused himself for the evening, Traynord exiting at the same time. Even after the young men had left the room, Sir Charles stood looking after them. Then he turned slowly and said, "I know you are all anxious for Freddy's safe return as, indeed, I am. I mislike exceedingly telling you that I do not know how it is to be effected."

There was a quick babble of voices which fell away when he lifted his hand. "You will not understand, I fear, why I cannot meet the demands of him—or them—whose writing this is." He held up the note, allowing them to regard it for a moment. Then he sighed deeply and folded the paper into a small square.

"But, Papa!" Corinna protested. "Of course you will pay the ransom they ask. Otherwise they may do as they threaten." She threw an arm around Harriet, who was weeping softly. "These two girls have been thrown into a pucker; come, dear Papa, tell them that Freddy will be returned within not more than four-and-twenty hours."

"I cannot." He had been clinging to the back of a chair which he turned around so that he might sink into it. "This is most awkward for me to say," and he cast a worried look at his wife. "The truth of the matter is that I do not have ten thousand pounds."

The bald statement struck them in various ways. Rosalind and Harriet were incredulous, simply unable to accept his amazing avowal as the truth. Corinna stood shaking her head, gazing at her father as though he had taken leave of his senses. Lady Mary, a moment ago unable to lift her head from the back of the divan, sat up and looked at her husband with deep loathing.

"This must be one of your tricks, Bannestock," she said in a ringing voice. "I have encountered them before when you decide upon a pinch-penny policy. Ten thousand pounds! Indeed, you are worth a hundred times that

much and do not gainsay me on that head! When we were
married—"

"That is past history! It takes every penny of my in-
come to maintain this house, the servants, the stables,
new gowns at every turn for you and Corinna. And then
there were Mama's debts. I was honor bound to pay
them. Until the next quarter, Madam, there will be nothing to spare; certainly I could not find ten thousand
pounds to throw to criminals who may or may not keep
their promise to return Freddy to his home."

Never had Rosalind heard him speak in such a
hopeless and agonized manner. She could sense his humiliation at having to confess that his fortune was not all that
they had believed it to be and that there was no way for
him to free his nephew, who was the heir to the Bannestock title. She longed to go to him and put her arms about
him, for despite everything, he had been good to her and
her brother and sister.

But it was Corinna who reached his side first. She
picked up his hand and held it between her two, and she
said soothingly, "Do not let yourself be worried, dear
Papa. We shall manage to find the money some way.
What about our jewelry—Mama's and mine? Surely there
are pieces among it which are of great value. I am only
sorry we cannot find the rose pin, for I should like to give
it back to you so that you might raise enough money for
your needs."

Lady Mary, fanning herself vigorously with her handkerchief, sat up straighter and glared at the two. "What a
famous idea!" she said with great sarcasm. "You would
strip me of the few gewgaws I possess, some of them
given to me by my dear Papa many years ago. No, I shall
not permit that, not if Freddy . . ."

She seemed to realize that she had gone too far and fell
back, mumbling to herself. Sir Charles said tenderly to his
daughter, "Thank you, my love. You have a kind heart
and a generous spirit, but even every bauble owned by
you and your mother would not bring in the required
amount. One receives only a fraction of its worth when

selling jewelry. It is too bad, but it is so. I have lost quite a bit on the exchange, but that can be retrieved in time though not, I fear, in the near future."

Rosalind imagined Freddy confined to some dark and dangerous place and began to weep silently. How miserable life had become during the past few days! Before this big worry, there had been nibbling at the corner of her mind another one. She did not know the results of the encounter between Sir Julian and Willton Turncroft after she had revealed to the former what she had seen and heard at the Silver Crown.

As for Sir Julian, Corinna was mentioning his name ". . . asked me this very day," she said. "If I give him permission, he will speak to you and offer his hand. He is known to be one of the wealthiest men in London and with the marriage settlements . . ."

The atmosphere in the yellow drawing room changed drastically with Corinna's announcement that she would accept Sir Julian's offer of marriage. Her mother leaped from the sofa where she had been near-recumbent and with surprising agility ran to her daughter and embraced her.

"Oh, my darling girl!" she cried rapturously. "You will be the envy of every young woman in town, to say nothing of how much chagrin the announcement will cause in the bosoms of matchmaking mamas. I cannot wait for it to be known that you have captured the greatest matrimonial prize of all! We shall have a ball for you and dear Julian. Yes! And I shall send the notice to the newspapers . . ."

Her voice dwindled away and the light died from her face when she became aware of the sobriety with which her daughter and Sir Charles were regarding her.

"This miserable business about Freddy is spoiling everything," she complained then. "So long I have waited for you two young people to realize you were meant for each other! Bannestock!" She turned to her husband. "Somehow you must manage to have your important discussion with Julian as soon as possible. He will be generous, I know, where the settlement is concerned. Then we may be happy again."

Rosalind could not have said how she was feeling. Torn in two directions, she was thankful that the money to release Freddy would be forthcoming; but that Corinna and Sir Julian would become man and wife was like a sharp, unremitting pain inside her.

She slid a glance in Harriet's direction and saw that her sister was sitting quietly gazing at her hands, clasped in her lap. What, she wondered, was Harriet thinking at this moment? After Rosalind's rosy plans for her, she must be bitterly disappointed, perhaps even resentful because her hopes had been raised and then shattered.

"And so," Lady Mary said, as though making a great concession, "we must wait until that annoying boy returns home before we can proceed with the plans for the ball. But come," and she held out her hand to her daughter, "and we shall go up to your chamber and make a list of what you will need for your trousseau."

In her triumphant mood, she was able to spare a few gracious words for her husband's nieces. "There will be much social activity here from now on. Tomorrow will be time enough, I do believe, for you to look over some of Corinna's old gowns, which Biggers may be able to refurbish for you both."

Not a word about Freddy, Rosalind thought, more in sadness than anger. Not a thought about the fact that his safety depended upon the sum of money Sir Charles could inveigle out of his daughter's future husband.

Harriet hurried out of the room, the same sort of agitation seeming to be evident on her face; and when Sir Charles left, too, Rosalind was left alone in the room where all her hopes for her sister had come crashing down.

As she was crossing the room on her way to the door, she saw that the letter which Sir Charles had read to them had dropped from his hand and was lying on the floor in front of the fireplace. She stooped and picked it up. She read it slowly, every word imprinting itself on her mind. "If you wish to see your nephew alive, you will have to pay for his return. We have him as a prisoner . . ."

Something puzzled her. Something wrinkled her forehead with a frown. She did not know why this letter, written on the cheapest of paper, struck a false note. It was what one would expect to have been written by someone of little education, and yet it seemed to have been designed for just that purpose. Simple words were misspelled, and longer ones were spelled correctly. Punctuation was both good and bad. She folded the piece of paper carefully and put it in the pocket of her skirt. She planned to examine it more closely at some future time. At this moment, she wanted to be with Harriet, whose heartbreak must be the most painful of all.

17

She found Harriet in their bedchamber, mending a skirt which had become ragged along its hem. There was a faint aura of sadness about her, but she was far from cast down and Rosalind thought that whatever her sister was feeling, she was managing to keep it well hidden.

Rosalind hesitated about bringing up the subject of Corinna's coming betrothal to Sir Julian, for Harriet might be thrown into a pucker. Their plan for ensnaring the young baronet had proved to be a dreadful failure. But it was Harriet herself who introduced that subject into the conversation.

"I should have known that never could I stand beside her for all things. She is of the sweetest nature, to say nothing of being a diamond of the first water. Yes, she and Sir Julian will deal well, I am sure." She let a tiny sigh escape from her lips. "It seems, does it not, that they were made for each other."

Her curiosity too great to be denied. Rosalind asked, "Do you not care at all, my dear one? After a twelve-month of feeling a *tendre* for him, are you not shattered to find he has attached himself to someone else?"

"Yes, but I know now that it was nothing more than a silly dream. I am not the kind who would make an acceptable wife for Sir Julian," she admitted freely. "Had he offered for me instead of Corinna, I should have been overjoyed to accept. But it was not to be, sister, and so I must put aside my idiotish dreams and accept the fact that I shall dwindle into an old maid." When Rosalind tried to speak, Harriet shook her head. "With all this going on about Freddy, how could either of us concern ourselves with anything else? Oh, Rosalind, do you really think he will come back? I fear I shall not close an eye this night worrying and waiting for news of him."

"We will hear tomorrow. Then when Sir Julian settles the marriage portion matter and there is money to pay the abductors, we shall have Freddy back safe and sound."

Not letting Harriet see her face lest it betray her, Rosalind picked up her own sewing bag and wished that she had given Harriet reassurance when she herself felt so little.

The second letter came late the next afternoon. In spite of the fact that two footmen had been on watch from a kitchen window all that day in hopes of catching the kidnapper in the act of delivering the anticipated note, they had seen nothing on the street but the usual passersby: young ladies going shopping in their finery or to join the Bond Street stroll, a lad sweeping a crossing, a man beating his horse as it pulled a heavy cart over the cobblestones.

Whoever had slipped the letter under the front door had not been seen. This time the address on the envelope read: "Miss Rosalind Bannestock"—another mystery.

They had all been having tea in one of the smaller drawing rooms, including Sir Julian who would, once the amenities had been observed, likely be closeted in Sir Charles's book room to discuss the financial arrangements of the coming marriage. There had been a short space of time when the baronet and Corinna had been alone and everyone in the house imagined what was taking place behind the closed door.

When they emerged and joined the others, neither had the rapturous look of a pair madly in love. Corinna looked tense and nerve ridden; Sir Julian was his usual urbane self, but his easy smile was missing.

Then, just as they were finishing tea, Haybolt had come in holding the letter by one corner as though it contained some infectious material and said in a voice which sounded as though he were pronouncing the heralding of doom, "For you, Miss Rosalind."

"Why," she wondered aloud, "was it sent to me?" She tore the corner of the envelope and drew out the sheet of paper inside with dread.

The letter read: "You may prepare to welcome your brother, Frederick Bannestock. As soon as you have paid the ten thousand pounds, he will be restored to you." High-flown language Rosalind thought but did not call the attention of the others to the precise way everything was set forth. "You and you alone must deliver the money. No one except your family must know of your errand."

Dismayed, she stopped reading and looked about at the others. All of them were leaning forward in their chairs as though not wishing to miss a single word. She began to read again.

"If you notify the Runners of anything that is written down here, it will mean that your brother will die. You are to put the money in a shoe box and leave it at a place which will be designated at the bottom of this page. Do not forget: Any news that leaks out will mean that Frederick Bannestock will die!"

As her voice stopped abruptly, the others sat as though stunned. Even Lady Mary was bereft of words. Her eyes blinked but there was no movement in any other part of her body.

Sir Charles finally said, "Go on, my dear. There is more I am sure."

She turned over the sheet of paper. The writing there was harder to read for the lines criss-crossed. "Freddy is

being held at a spot near Sussex but that is all you need
to know."

Directions were then given for reaching a certain
crossroads on the way to Sussex, where Rosalind was to
repair to as quickly as possible to drop the money which
she was to wrap in a heavy sheet of paper. Then she was
to go away quickly and not linger in the hopes of seeing
who would retrieve the package.

There was a great babble of voices. Harriet begged her
sister not to chance her life on what might be a fool's errand. Lady Mary, ignored and pouting over that fact,
muttered that she did not know what the world was coming to. Matthew held one of Harriet's hands in his and
patted it vigorously when she began to weep.

There was no sense in even discussing the matter, Sir
Charles declared. He would not, he vowed, allow a niece
of his to venture forth on a dark road at this time of the
evening. They must all forget what the letter had contained. He would find another way of bringing Freddy
back to safety. Corinna and Sir Julian, looking much subdued, had little to say.

In the midst of the hubbub, Rosalind managed to slip
upstairs. Let them say what they would, advance any arguments they chose, nothing would prevent her from carrying out the instructions which would bring Freddy back
to them.

It was easier to face them when she was garbed in her
riding dress. Not that they didn't try to dissuade her from
setting out on the dangerous errand. But she refused to
listen to their arguments, and facing Sir Julian, she said,
"I believe you have the bank notes in the amount of ten
thousand pounds. Will you not make up the package as
ordered in the letter so that I may be on my way?"

What a courageous little creature she was! he thought.
With no regard for her own safety she would set out alone
and ride a dark and dangerous road without an outward
qualm.

He bowed and went with Sir Charles to the book room
to make up the package. When they returned, Harriet was

weeping quietly on Matthew's shoulder; Lady Mary, much recovered, was mourning the days of her girlhood when young ladies were garbed as they should be at certain times of the day; and Corinna was gazing moodily into the fireplace.

Rosalind did not doubt but that she was starting off on her journey alone. She did not know that she was to be followed by three horsemen, each leaving separately to make his own journey to the specified crossroads on the way to Sussex.

As soon as the door had closed behind Rosalind Sir Julian excused himself hastily. Within a matter of minutes, he was mounted and giving his horse his head, straining his eyes for the sight of the mild-mannered bay which Rosalind had been riding on the day she had discovered Corinna and Sir Willton in the Silver Crown.

Sir Charles, making known his intentions to ride to protect his niece, found himself, much surprised, the target of a bitter tirade by Freddy's tutor.

"Sir, I can consider such a course of action the greatest of folly. You heard, of course, the warning that if others were to be apprised of the abduction, it would not go well with their captive." Matthew's face was of a scarlet hue and his Adam's apple sped up and down at an alarming rate. Yet he held his ground even in the face of Sir Charles's burgeoning anger. "You would be jeopardizing not only the life of your nephew, but also that of an intrepid young woman the like of whom one seldom has the good fortune to meet."

At this point, Harriet slid away from him, though he did not seem to notice. With his chin trembling only slightly, he went on speaking ringingly.

"Care you so little for this remarkable young lady that you would, with not a qualm, do what you were warned not to do even though it might mean the death of two whom you should love dearly?"

The three women in the room held their breaths as they waited for the outburst that must surely come. But

Sir Charles merely threw a contemptuous look in the direction of his nephew's tutor and shrugged.

"I cannot remember when it was said that I must take such talk from one in your position, Traynord. When I return we shall talk on that head. I am sure, even without a character from me, you will manage to find work elsewhere."

Harriet cried in a tiny voice, "Oh, no, Uncle Charles!" and Corinna said, with great sense, "It is not the time to speak of things like that, not when we are all in a pucker. The important thing now is that we bring them both home safely."

She fastened upon her father a long, sympathetic glance. "Yes, dear Papa, as their guardian I think you are feeling just as you ought and must go in pursuit of poor, dear Rosalind."

Sir Charles was much cheered by having Corinna on his side and went upstairs to change into riding clothes. By the time he had done so and the groom had saddled his favorite mount, many minutes had passed and the task of overtaking Rosalind seemed hopeless.

No sooner was he gone than Matthew took his leave, putting Harriet determinedly away from him in spite of her pleas that he remain.

"I must do my part to rescue this lady who means so much to me!" he said in ringing tones. "I can hide my feelings for her no longer. She has captured my heart as you must all know and the thought of her falling into the hands of unscrupulous blackguards is more than I can bear! Unworthy as I am, I have no aspirations of her accepting my hand for she is far above my touch but if I can render her assistance at this time of her greatest need, I shall count the day the luckiest in my entire existence. Pray do not try to prevail upon me to sit idly by when she has need of my assistance."

It was the longest and most impassioned speech any of them had heard from him. Harriet sprang away from him as though she had been stung. Lady Mary pursed her little mouth and murmured something about his having been correct in his statement about being unworthy, and gave him a dim and approving smile.

Owning no horse of his own, he was obliged to hire a job horse, and it was very late before he took the path the others had chosen, part of him resentful because Sir Julian would undoubtedly be the first to overtake her, the other a bittersweet happiness because his loved one would be defended, if need be, by a nonpareil skilled at sword play, a boxer second to none and a true shot if, indeed, he had firearms on his person.

At that moment Sir Julian was not planning to use, in the very near future, his pistol, his sword or his fists. It was fate which had decreed otherwise.

He was hopelessly lost on a side road, not many miles from Sussex, he judged, having taken a wrong turn some miles back. In vain he had searched for a signpost but if there were such anywhere about, it was swallowed up by the darkness. He was exceedingly irked and cursed the circumstances which had put him in this position, not only because it was of utmost importance that he find Rosalind but also because it was humiliating to have lost his way like the veriest schoolboy.

Now he turned his horse around and started down the road in the direction from which he had come—or so he believed.

Nor had Sir Charles had much better luck. His horse had thrown a shoe before he was out of the city and it was necessary for him to find a stable before he could proceed.

Only Matthew made the ride without mishap and he, unfortunately, did not know where he was going.

18

From the time that Rosalind had read the second let-
ter, she had been aware of Freddy's whereabouts. Having
lived her girlhood years in Sussex, she knew most of its
landmarks. Close to the spot where she was to leave the
payment for Freddy's return, there was a small outbuilding, scarcely more than a rude shack. She tied her horse
to a tree some distance from it and then hid the package
in a clump of bushes, covering it carefully with dried
leaves.

Then, walking on tiptoe so that the sound of her footsteps on the littered path would not be heard, she approached the little outbuilding from the rear. There were
no windows there and so she went quietly to the side of
the shack, where there were a pair of glass panes so dusty
she could scarcely see through them.

Carefully so that she would not be seen by whatever
occupants were inside, she took out a handkerchief and
rubbed a spot on the window which gave her a view of an
ill-furnished room. A horse tethered at a fence in front of
the shack whinnied and threw back his head so that his
harness jingled. She flattened herself against the wall,

hoping that she might discover who was inside before her presence was noted.

No one came out and she took her place again at the window. In her line of vision was a man whose age, she judged, from his back, the set of his shoulders and the thick hair which fell to the nape of his neck, must be no more than a few years greater than hers.

There came upon her a feeling of having done before exactly what she was doing at this minute: gazing in through a window at this man in the room beyond. And, she saw when he turned and she could catch a glimpse of his face, it *was* the very same man!

Sir Willton Turncroft, who had on that other occasion been arguing with Corinna in a room in the Silver Crown, was now evidently doing the very same thing with someone who was beyond her view.

She could not hear what he was saying, for unlike the other occasion the window was closed. And so she could see only the movement of Sir Willton's mouth and the ugly expression upon his face. Could what she was thinking actually be true? She could not believe that this young man, highly born as he was and with a title already in spite of his young years, would do something as criminal as abduction when there seemed to be no possible reason for such a course of action.

Yet she was forced to believe it, for as she moved from that window to another one, she could see Freddy seated on a crude chair with ropes around his ankles and waist to tether him where he sat. There was another man in the room and although Rosalind's vision was somewhat cut off she could see enough of him to realize that he, too, was tied to his chair while Sir Willton walked between the two, his mouth going at a great rate of speed and his countenance seeming to grow more angry by the minute. At one point when he approached Freddy with his fist raised, she was certain that he meant to strike the boy.

But he did not. And now she could follow his line of reasoning. The boy was his trump card. By keeping Freddy captive, he knew that the balance of power was on his side. The Bannestocks must submit to his demands or lose the boy who had been a member of their household these twelve months and more.

But why, she wondered as she gazed into that lighted room, did Sir Willton have need of money? The Turncroft fortune was said to be an exceedingly impressive one. True, she had believed that Sir Charles was wealthy beyond all things and had discovered how wrong she had been in so believing. Yet something seemed to tell her that this abduction of Freddy was not an ordinary one. She remembered how Sir Willton had tried to court her and attach himself to Harriet also; and there had been the time, not very long ago, when he had sought Freddy's friendship by allowing him to drive his cattle.

Rosalind's impulse was to flee, but she remained staring into the room as though to imprint upon her mind every sadly shabby stick of furniture in it, appalled that Freddy must have spent at least four-and-twenty hours in such wretched surroundings. She knew that she must not be foolhardy if she were to lead him to safety, and as she stood there she tried to plan the best way to proceed. The other man tied to a chair could not help her in the present situation; she wondered about him, where he fit into the picture, how he came to be bound like a trussed chicken, when he looked as though he were rough enough and sufficiently strong to take care of himself under any circumstances.

He was a man close to middle age and his clothing was shabby. He had a blunt-featured face, his eyebrows thick and black and bristly. His hands were crossed and bound at the wrists—great, blunt-fingered hands which looked as though they could choke the life out of a human body without much trouble. But now he was helpless, and the scowl which lay across his forehead was deep and dark.

She must go for help, she knew. There was no way at all, alone as she was, that she could do anything to help Freddy and his fellow victim—for that she thought the elder man must be—without assistance from someone. She had covered many miles since she had left Grosvenor

Square. The time mentioned in the demanding letter was close at hand.

The letter. There was something about the memory of those criss-crossed lines which perturbed her. Never having seen Sir Willton's handwriting she could not know whether or not he had been the one who had written the note. Of one thing she was growing more and more certain as she drew into her mind a picture of those written words.

The handwriting very much resembled Freddy's.

Puzzlement made her careless. She turned to run to the place where she had tethered her horse and under her feet cracked a little nest of dried twigs and when she jumped away from them she lost her balance and landed in a bush. Its sharp branches scraped along her cheek and she cried out an exclamation of pain, and somehow she was heard, for the door of the little shack opened. There was a flare of candles and then she saw Sir Willton not more than a hundred yards away from her.

In the darkness she could not see his face very plainly but she could feel his eyes upon her and she took a few steps backward, fearing with each one that she would fall for she was moving into darkness, and having lost her sense of direction, not sure that she was going in the right one.

There was no moon and the candle which the man held in his hand flickered weakly. But there was enough light for her to see that Sir Willton had something in his other hand—an ugly-looking pistol.

The two left behind in the outbuilding began to shout; she could hear their voices breaking the silence. They cried for help in the hope that whoever had found the place where they were held prisoners had come to rescue them.

Rosalind moved farther back and her foot struck a boulder behind her. She lost her balance for a moment or two but managed to regain it and skirted around the large rock. She would have run in the direction of her horse, but she saw that such a course was impossible, for she could see the light of Sir Willton's candle, and he was standing between her and the horse.

She turned and ran back to the shack. Its door stood open and she ran over the splintery threshold and fell on her knees beside her brother. She gave no thought to the dusty floor or that she could not take him comfortably into her arms. But she was able to look into his face and say soothingly, "Dear Freddy! You must not worry. We shall soon have you out of this scrape. But tell me—how does it come about that I find you in such a place as this with that odious man?"

She turned her head and threw a look of loathing at the young nobleman who stood lounging in the doorway.

"He shall, of course, pay for this despicable deed, for I have no doubt that the others will come soon, finding this place as I have found it. I pray you will believe me when I tell you what this wretched man has done. He has demanded a great sum of money—ten thousand pounds—for your return. But he shall not receive a single penny!"

She thought of the package hidden near the place where she had tied her horse. The money had not seemed too much to bring Freddy back to his family, but now that she had discovered that her brother was alive, and that no harm would come to him now that she had discovered the perpetrator of the crime, she was determined that Sir Willton Turncroft would not be paid anything at all.

Freddy was wearing a most peculiar expression. It was not fear, not in its usual sense at least. It seemed more like uneasiness, as though the ropes which bound him were not causing him as much distress as something inside him.

Sir Willton, who had stiffened when she made her reassuring statement about Freddy's rescuers, now came into the room, crossed it and was looking down at the two.

"What is it that you have said? Whom are you expecting? Who knows of the whereabouts of this odious little whelp?" he demanded. "How, in fact, did you find this place?"

She gazed up into the face above hers. "From the letter, of course. Did you not give instructions as to where to leave the money? How else would we have known?" She got to her feet and faced him without flinching. "What puzzles me deeply is what need you have of ten thousand pounds, a man of great wealth as you are. Now, sir, if you will untie these two, we shall be on our way. Perhaps," she said graciously, "we shall let the matter drop once we are back home. It may be that Sir Charles will consent to overlook your dastardly crime if you can persuade him that it was merely a lighthearted prank, the work of a bored man about town."

He had been listening to her carefully, and now he said, "Tell me more about this letter you claimed to have received, why it was written, what it said. I am all in the dark, you see. I know not the slightest thing about what you are accusing me of."

There was a ring of truth in his voice. She turned to look again at Freddy, who had the grace to flush and look away. Then she turned her glance on the other man who was tied to his chair and asked softly, "Had you not better tell me the truth, Frederick Bannestock. Who is this person? What is his name?"

Freddy returned sullenly, "He is called Jim. That is all you need know. He is my friend."

"Indeed not. You must tell me the whole story. Where have you been and why do you cry friends with someone who—who is of such a different ilk as yourself?" It was the most civil way she could think of to point out the disparity in their stations. It did not lower him in her eyes that his clothing was shabby and unfashionable, for she had never been high in the instep, but she was genuinely interested in why Freddy had become the companion of a man whom he would not ordinarily have met in the natural course of affairs. "Where did you meet?"

"In the city where I had gone to search for Molly." His voice was so low that it could scarcely be heard, and both Sir Willton and Rosalind leaned closer to him to hear what he was saying. "Jim is—well, it is not necessary for you to know each separate thing about him. But he, as I myself, mislikes exceedingly the conditions in which poor wretches must live in the city. As I have said before, many of them starve to death with no one to care."

"But Freddy, dear," Rosalind said mildly, "there is little one person can do. Do you not believe that if such had been the case, Harriet and I would have tried to make their lot lighter? But there seemed to be no way . . ."

"There is a way! People should be willing to sacrifice some of their luxuries," he said fiercely, "to the task of seeing poor people fed and decently clothed! And to see that their health is at least the concern of those who could help them. That is why . . ." and he fell silent.

Poor Freddy! Rosalind thought. He had taken to his heart the plight of all those who suffered.

"And so," she said in great sympathy, "you concocted this scheme to get money from Uncle Charles. It was you who wrote those two letters, pretending to have been abducted. It was your writing, although you tried to disguise it."

He was much like herself, she thought with sudden wisdom. He made foolish plans which never came to fruition. He found himself in scrapes exactly as she did, and now she understood most of what had happened in the past days, but there was something which still puzzled her.

"What part has Sir Willton in this escapade? Why do I find him here with a firearm in his hand?"

She turned to look at him, but he returned the glance with a bland smile. Jim, who at intervals tried to pull out of his bonds, made a growling sound deep in his throat. Freddy, at that moment, seemed too angry to speak.

It was Sir Willton himself who gave the explanation. "Dear Miss Rosalind, it can be told in simple terms. I happened to espy these two rogues in the city and followed them here. Luckily I was armed and, in the circumstances, it was not difficult to force them to tell me what they were up to. They led me to this place which, I will own, is not the acme of luxury." He shrugged carelessly.

"I find it most suitable for my purposes just as they considered it ideal for theirs."

"And that is?"

"Can you not guess?" His face, which she had never considered attractive, now seemed to have taken on a look of malevolence so strong it was almost frightening. His eyes gleamed with a light of animallike greed. She took an involuntary step backward.

"Are you such a widgeon that you thought I was seeking you out having been attracted by your charms or those of your whey-faced sister, Long Peg that she is? Or honestly wished to take your repellent little brother up in my carriage? I wanted nothing except that one thing you have which I coveted as I have never done anything else."

His expression had changed. Rosalind might have been looking at a man feeling the pain of unrequited love. "From the first moment my eyes touched upon it, I have wanted nothing in the world except that lovely, desirable little pin designed as a rose."

19

"You are all about in your head," Rosalind said in a voice which caught in her throat. "First of all, the pin does not belong to me. It is Corinna's. Along with that . . ."

She broke off the sentence as she remembered that the valuable little object was missing, a fact which she did not want to divulge at this time. Sir Willton's knowing of that would serve no purpose except, perhaps, to raise his anger. And they were completely at his mercy, and as his hand caressed his pistol, he was like a man overtaken by a great longing, seeing in his mind the piece of jewelry he so deeply desired.

In a tone which rose and fell, he went on speaking of the object of his desire. "I saw it, you see, when my mother and I called upon Sir Charles's mother some years ago. It is famous; having gazed upon it when she showed it to us with great pride in her manner, I could not get it out of my mind. Although I was never to see it again, I spent hours thinking about it and wishing that it were mine."

Rosalind thought that he must be telling the truth. No doubt there were men who were possessed by great desires to own something: a work of art, a woman, a certain piece of land. And being denied what they wanted most in the world, were willing to commit crimes—even to kill, perhaps—to bring it into their possession.

Oddly, she felt a little sorry for Sir Willton. And his discourse was allowing her to realize certain things.

"When your grandmother died, I knew my beloved little pin went to you, Miss Rosalind, as it went to all ladies with 'rose' somewhere in their names. You see, I have studied my subject well. From the time I first saw it and knew that one day it would belong to me, I have learned as much as I could about it."

"No, no, Sir Willton, you must listen to me." With much urgency in her voice and face, she tried to persuade him that the little pin was not hers and never had been. "It was not given to me, sir. My uncle, instead, bestowed it upon Corinna, telling her that his mother would so have wanted. I vow to you that I did not so much as hold that piece of jewelry in my hand at any time."

"It will serve you nothing to lie." He was becoming disagreeable again. "So pitch me no gammon, if you please. I know that you are holding in your possession what I have always felt must be meant for me since I have this great desire for it. Sir Charles break with tradition? I am not so hen-witted as to believe that!"

"It is true, nevertheless," she insisted, although she despaired of making him believe her.

She could imagine him as a boy; he would have had indulgent parents, nursemaids, governesses and tutors who would make sure that there was no thing, no matter how small or large, which he could not have if he so desired. Never had he been denied his slightest wish—except when he had fallen in love with a little article of jewelry which belonged to someone else. So overwhelming was his desire to own it that he would do anything—hold innocent people at the point of a gun, steal, cheat, lie—to have his own way. And murder? Rosalind wondered, her blood seeming to freeze. Would he kill them all if he thought it would bring into his possession what he so deeply coveted?

"If you will not believe me, there is no way for me to persuade you." She felt fluttery inside but managed to pretend calmness. "Sir Charles, you see, has been away on business. When he returned, he discovered the theft. Someone was luckier than the burglar you hired and sent earlier."

There, she had let the secret be known and had not intended to do so. For she had some half-formed idea that she might be able to bargain with him; to tell him that if he would release Freddy and his friend, she would make an attempt to have Sir Charles put a price on the little piece of jewelry with the intention of selling it.

At any rate it did not matter what she had blurted out. Sir Willton was regarding her with a mocking smile. "Doing it much too brown, Miss Rosalind. I cannot blame you for concocting a Banbury tale, and I must needs compliment your guile. You speak of a theft as casually as though it were nothing at all. Am I to take it that you wish me to believe that the rose pin is no longer in your possession? That it has been stolen?"

"And never was in my possession, sir!"

"It will not wash." He shook his head decisively. "Sir Charles would *not* break with tradition. That would be the shabbiest of tricks. Tell me," he asked curiously, "what made you think I would swallow a story like that? Am I such a gudgeon as to have wool pulled over my eyes?"

"I was not trying to do so, Sir Willton." Her hands were clasped, and she thought that surely he must believe that she was speaking the truth for she was not a good liar and her Papa had often said that she had no success with even the smallest of fibs. "On the day Sir Charles returned home, it was discovered that the pin was missing. Everything else was locked away in a strong box except that, which belonged there also. No one knew what had become of it. My uncle questioned each of us and the servants as well. To make matters worse, a kitchen maid named Molly . . ."

She glanced apologetically at Freddy, who was straining against the ropes which bound him. She knew that the pleading in his face meant that he wanted her to say no more.

"I am sorry, dear brother. I know you believe her innocent. But," she explained, "I am trying to convince Sir Willton that there was a theft and that one of the servants is missing. If he will only take that into his mind, he will know that I speak the truth and that there is some explanation for what has happened."

Freddy burst out fiercely, "Do you not see what you have done? Now you have marked poor Molly as a thief. This bounder here, money enough and above, can hunt her down and torture her into telling him where that wretched geegaw is, if she knows, which I swear she does not."

"Have you seen her?" Rosalind asked eagerly. "Was it for her you wanted the ten thousand pounds or part of it?"

He shook his head sullenly in answer to one of the questions and confessed reluctantly to the truth of the other. "There are so many like her, and I hoped to relieve some of their misery."

"There! And so you shall." She patted his tousled hair soothingly. "When you are a little older you can do much on the lines you wish. Now let us get home for the others will be fretting and worried."

She turned to Sir Willton and said more pleasantly than she felt, "Now if you will be so obliging as to untie the ropes that bind Freddy and his friend, we shall be on our way. Since there is but the one horse between the three of us, and you, I would suppose, have only yours and no rig to accommodate us, Jim and Freddy will have to take turns riding behind me. Poor animal! After the long journey, he has had no care. As soon as we reach the first posting house . . ."

She glanced at Sir Willton in surprise, for he had not

moved from the spot where he had been standing and was making no attempt to hide the fact that he did not intend to do as she had requested.

Annoyed, she took a step toward her brother but Sir Willton stepped into her path and blocked the way. His face was uglier than she had ever seen it and she began to feel a little frightened. Her voice trembled as she said, "Kindly let me pass. I shall untie the ropes myself."

"You cannot do so without a sharp blade. I will set them free when it so pleases me."

"Then let that time be now! We have a long journey, many miles to cover and cannot reach home now until the morning, I fear. Sir Willton, I beg of you let us finish this foolishness. You have failed to do what you hoped to. And you have taken advantage of a young boy's folly so cannot you accept that there is no way at all for you to achieve what you set out to do? May we not bid each other good night without further quarreling?"

"How simple you make it sound!" he sneered. "I am to let you go on your way and turn your back on the whole matter. You must know by now what I wish for above all things on earth. Do you think I would give up so easily? Yes, your brother and his friend may leave. I shall cut the ropes at once . . ."

Her thankful cry interrupted him. "Oh, Sir Willton, I thank you for your kindness! And none shall ever know what went on here this night. Never a word of it shall pass my lips and they, too," nodding in the direction of the other two, "will never speak of it to anyone. Come, free them, and we will all be out of this wretched place."

He did not move an inch from where he was standing. Her voice began to falter. "Sir Willton? Come, it is very late. We are causing those at home to worry."

"You think I care at all for that?"

"I do not know," she returned candidly, "what goes on in your head, sir. I know only that I could not give you the rose pin even if I wished to do so. However, since you feel as you do about it, perhaps, when it is found, Corinna will allow you to see it, even take it into your hands for she is a good-hearted girl and I am persuaded that . . ."

"Do not pitch me such gammon!" He seemed to suddenly grow even angrier. "I mean to have it for my own, do you not understand that? And, yes, your brother and his friend may be on their way. But you and I, Madam, will remain until they are far enough away."

She cried, confused, "But I do not know what you are talking about! I shall, of course, go with Freddy."

"Indeed you will not! I have decided that you are to remain with me this night. Oh, do not worry your head," and he laughed an ugly laugh as she stepped back and away from him. "It is not you with whom I am in love. To me you are merely a bartering point. Surely now you understand. Your loving brother can carry the message to Sir Charles. When the pin is in my hands, you will be allowed to return home. In the meantime—well, you can imagine what will happen to your name if it is known that you spent the night with me."

Freddy began to make outraged sounds in his throat and thrash about so that he managed to move his chair a few inches. But strain against the ropes as he would, he could not free himself. Even Jim, a glowering, phlegmatic man, looked outraged. He spoke for the first time since Rosalind had come into the shanty.

"I've met the dregs of humanity in me time," he growled, "but none as low as you, matey. Nobleman, indeed! It's a black soul you have. Ye'd ruin the name of an innocent lass as easy-like as you'd step on an insect just to get your hands on a frippery piece of jewelry. It's what you are saying, is it?"

Sir Willton said coolly, "You have grasped my meaning, fool! Congratulations upon having a few wits. I shall allow you to find your way home. There will be few people on the road at dawn. Then, when you have reached London, you will explain to Sir Charles how the land lies."

He spoke now to Freddy, whose face had taken on a crimson hue as his anger mounted. "You will bring back that beautiful little object and your sister will be set free. If you follow my orders and all goes well, we shall complete our bargain before another day has ended. If you do not . . ."

"I shall never be part of your nefarious scheme!" Freddy burst out. "You have heard what my sister has said. The little gewgaw is missing. How could I possibly follow orders of that sort, even if I would consent to do so?"

Sir Willton looked at him with icy hatred. "If you interrupt me again, young sir, it will be worse for you. What I am trying to make you understand is that if you all follow my plan, no one will be hurt or disgraced. If you are not willing to do so, then it shall be as I told you. The young lady will be released in due time, I shall spread the word as to where she has been, and if you are not completely dim-witted, you know what that will mean! I shall give you twenty-four hours in which to return with the pin, and not a second more."

She and Freddy exchanged anguished glances. They were a confession that it was futile to hope that there was any way out of this tangle. The pin could not be delivered to Sir Willton because no one knew where it was. And if he carried out his threat—as they were sure he would—it would mean ruination for her. She could not help wishing that Sir Willton's hired burglar had not failed in his attempt to steal the pin; then all this trouble would not have befallen her.

20

Freddy spoke through gritted teeth. "*If you do this,*
Willton, I shall kill you! Someday, somehow, I shall find
great pleasure in running my blade through your body. It
may take years but wherever you are I shall hunt you
down, and you will never make old bones, sir, that I
will promise you here and now."

For some reason Freddy's pronouncements did not
sound overdramatic. Rosalind's heart, as cold and hard as
stone until this minute, began to melt as she gazed upon
her brother's flushed and twisted features. Dear Freddy!
Under the blustering and superior attitude there was a
firm degree of love for his sisters.

Sir Willton still held the pistol in one hand and the
other was outstretched toward a knot in the rope which
bound Jim to his chair when they all heard, at the very
same moment, the sound coming from outside. It was an
unmistakable sound, one which they all recognized at
once: the pounding of a horse's hooves becoming louder
as it approached and then stopped outside the door of the
shack.

Sir Willton whirled, the gun aimed at the door which, to

the accompaniment of the horse's whinnying, flew suddenly open.

Rosalind could not believe her eyes. Standing there with the darkness of the night behind him was Matthew Traynord. His driving coat was dusty, his boots muddy; he was hatless and his hair was sadly tousled by the wind.

But his voice was strong and firm as he cried out, "So, I have found you, knave! Do you think you have surprised me with this dastardly deed?" Seeming not to notice the two men tied to their chairs, he rushed to Rosalind's side. "If you have harmed one hair on this lady's head, I shall kill you with my bare hands!"

He held them out and they looked white and delicate in the light of the candle. He seemed to be about to throw himself upon Sir Willton but evidently thought better of it with the pistol pointed directly at his heart. But his voice remained strong and furious.

"I do not know what has been going on here these past hours," he shouted, "but I fear the worst!"

His eyes fell upon Freddy and then upon the other man. He was beginning to feel uncertain.

Sir Willton said in a bored tone, "Then it seems I have a new adversary—the tutor. Take my advice, you fool, and go back to the schoolroom. This does not concern you."

"Anything," Matthew declaimed, "which concerns Miss Rosalind is of importance to me! Which you will discover if you will put down that thing you hold in your hand and let us be matched evenly—fists which are the weapons of nature."

He held his in front of his face and advanced slowly upon the baronet. "Unfortunately I am unarmed. But I beg of you to step outside where the battle may be fair. I am not as skilled as perhaps you are in fisticuffs but right is on my side and that, I believe, will help me to defeat you."

"Matthew!" Even Rosalind was beginning to feel a little impatient. "Do not be a gudgeon! You can see that he could shoot you without the least little bit of trouble. It is noble of you to want to rescue me but prosing will do no good and, as you can see, Sir Willton is pointing his pistol right at your heart. How, if I may ask you, do you think you can best him?"

The disparaging question seemed to urge him to action. He sprang forward and to one side, his fists still raised, and bumped into Sir Willton who, in turn, bumped into the seated Freddy who, chair and all, tumbled over backward.

Two bodies, and a third still tethered, made a heap of legs and arms flailing in all directions. Jim, reaching out in an attempt to assist his friend, went toppling over also.

Fearing that her brother who was on the bottom of the pile of squirming humanity would be seriously injured, Rosalind fluttered about, screaming. There were curses from Jim, grunting from Sir Willton who tried to extricate himself from the heap, a steady stream of gasped phrases from Matthew. Freddy was silent.

In the melee the pistol had slid from Sir Willton's hand and slid across the floor to a spot near Rosalind's feet. She gave a glad cry and stooped to pick it up. Guessing her intention, the baronet threw Matthew off him with a mighty heave. As Rosalind bent down, his head met hers in a collision and they both fell backward, breathless.

But he was able to struggle to where the firearm had fallen and she saw, as she pulled herself into a sitting position, that he had it in his possession once more.

During the set-to Freddy's bonds had come loose and he found himself free. But there was nothing he could do, for Sir Willton stood by the door now holding the pistol in a steady hand. And although Matthew, too, was on his feet and Jim, still cursing, was shaking himself free, there was nothing they could do for her or each other, not while Sir Willton was armed and they were not.

He made them line up against the further wall and fear suddenly began to spread through Rosalind's body like an icy spray. The encounter between the men had been such a debacle that she had lost sight of the fact that they were all facing certain death. Certainly he would not kill them all! Her heart began to ache for Freddy. So young, so little of his life lived and—despite everything—his good brain and tender conscience wasted.

"Can we not," she asked in a quavering voice, "make some sort of bargain? The pin is lost or stolen, at any rate it is missing. But there is a great deal of money in the bushes out yonder which was intended for the release of Freddy."

Her brother had the grace to look ashamed. "It was the worst of all schemes," he admitted. "All I intended . . ."

"It matters not a farthing what you intended," Sir Willton said sharply. "The money has no meaning for me if it will not buy what I want. Perhaps there is another way. I am persuaded there must be."

He bit upon his lower lip for a moment or two. Then he said thoughtfully, "It would not be to my credit were *I* to reveal that Miss Rosalind spent the night with me here. I should appear the veriest of bounders. People might even suspect that I held her against her will. No, that I will not do."

Then, after a short spell of silence, he smiled as though something brilliant had come into his mind.

"You three shall go home. I will allow you to take one horse only. Two can ride and, taking turns, another can walk. Thus it will take you so long to arrive anywhere, you will be able to do no harm. By the time you can report on Miss Rosalind's whereabouts it will be too late."

She was afraid to ask the question but knew that she must.

"And I? If you send Freddy and Matthew and—and Jim away, pray tell me what you intend to do with me."

"You will know soon enough." He smiled smugly, seeming to savor his secret with excessive enjoyment. Then, as though unable to keep it any longer, revealed it to the three motionless men in direct line with his pistol. He gloated, "The lady and I are about to embark upon a trip." He laughed aloud. "Within not more than five minutes, we shall be on our way to Gretna Green!"

When she looked back later upon that scene in the re-mote little shack among deep grass, shrubbery and leaf-burdened trees, it was like recalling an exceedingly horrible nightmare.

The sky was beginning to streak with the colors of dawn when they all moved out of the rude building into the knee-deep growth around it. The horses whinnied at the approach of the little group. Rosalind's gentle bay answered with neighing, and thus Sir Willton was able to learn its whereabouts. But he was not interested in that kindly old creature. His own spirited cattle would take them many miles until exchanged for one at a posting house along the Great Northern Road. The three men could take turns in riding the job horse Matthew had hired.

It was a confused nightmare. All three men mounted a protest which Sir Willton ignored with as much indiffer-ence as he displayed when threatened with the worst of reprisals should they come across him at any time in the future. Whippings, arrests, gunshots, being run through by swords—the threats left him as calm as though he had not heard them. With his own gun, he herded them to where the horse was tethered. Freddy sullenly chose to be the one to walk at the outset of their journey, bringing no pleasure to the hearts of the other two men by saying, "Since you are older than me, you will find the trip on foot much more fatiguing."

He turned for one last outburst. "You are not aware that we may meet someone before too many hours have passed. In early morning the road is not precisely deserted."

"And," Matthew put in, "I was not the only one who set out to find Freddy. It will be an exceedingly short time before Sir Charles and Julian Wickstead will find their way. And you are to be much pitied when that happens."

Sir Willton made a mocking bow. "Then it behooves us to hurry and set out on our journey. The distance to the border is a long one, though I cannot but believe that I shall find it most enjoyable in the company of the lady who is to be my wife."

That brought another stream of threats and angry exclamations from the three, but the baronet, seeming to enjoy himself enormously, laughed aloud, his whole body shaking with mirth, though the hand that held the pistol remained steady.

The nightmare still held her in its grip when she saw Matthew and Jim mount the lethargic old horse and Freddy grasp its reins. She could not believe any of it was real: Sir Willton untying his horse, motioning her to get upon the saddle, the closeness of his body as he mounted behind her.

Gretna Green! The very name struck fear into her soul. She had heard of the nefarious place, as had all girls her age. It was a place where marriages were performed for all who fled—eloped was the word—to it for that purpose. It was, to her innocent mind, a place which would put upon her name the stigma of scandal. Now she was being forced to go there by this odious, dangerous man; and she would bring disgrace and shame not only upon herself but upon all the members of the Bannestock family.

"Please!" she whispered. "Let us turn back. It is yet time to abandon this foolish scheme!"

Under the clopping of the horse's hooves, she could scarcely hear his voice. But although the words came faintly to her ears, she could understand them.

"I will do anything, even marry you if I must, if I can only get into my possession that beautiful little pin."

21

"*It will not be such an unhappy state of affairs,*"
he went on, his voice sounding as pleasant as she had
ever heard it. "I could have done much worse in choosing
a wife. Your spirits must be curbed, of course, but I shall
be able to take care of that."

He was speaking, she thought bitterly, as though he
were considering the purchase of a piece of horseflesh.
Marry him, indeed! She could think of nothing she wished
to do less. There was only one man in the world she
wished for a husband, and he was lost to her forever—if,
in truth, she had ever had the slightest chance of having
him.

"You will find me a complaisant mate," Sir Willton was
saying. "It will be necessary, of course, for you to present
me with an heir. For the title must remain in the family.
But after that is taken care of, we may please ourselves in
whatever way we choose. I do not, at this time, have a
connection with anyone, so you may rest easy on that
score. Never has the prospect of having a mistress seemed
as attractive to me as owning the rose pin. Once I have

obtained it, perhaps my mind will be freed for other things."

With the coming of daylight, she could see something of their surroundings. And in the distance there was a spiraling thread of smoke, barely discernible but causing a great leaping of hope to cheer her. There must be, not very far ahead of them, a posting house or tavern; and here, she was certain, there would be someone to whom she could appeal, tell the story of her abduction to the border.

In the early morning, a woman whom she guessed to be the wife of the tavern owner was tossing grain to a flock of hens in the sideyard. Rosalind drew a long breath, waiting for Sir Willton to check his horse, for certainly the beast, as well as themselves, needed sustenance. But he did not allow so much as a lagging of the horse and when she saw that he had no intention of stopping, Rosalind raised a hand and cried out to the woman.

She received a wave of the hand in response. Her words were snatched up and floated away by the wind. She had not understood at all, Rosalind thought in despair; she was evidently saying to herself that the ways of quality were indeed exceedingly strange. The two of them crowded on the back of one horse when, it was not to be doubted, they had a stable full of them wherever it was that they lived.

So they must go on, and to Rosalind the journey stretched out interminably. She was beginning to feel too tired to dwell upon her plight, and in spite of herself, her head had grown heavy and begun to nod. Having been awake all night, she could not keep from falling asleep.

But no more than five minutes later she was awake. What had roused her was Sir Willton's low-voiced curse and his slashing of his crop against the horse's back. The beast shot forward and began to gallop at a great rate of speed which, even then, did not satisfy the baronet, who kept urging him on. It was then that Rosalind realized they were being followed. She could hear the clopping of hooves behind them and tried to turn to see who was riding the horse.

They were overtaken at the next curve. Sir Julian Wickstead, known among his peers as a "bruising rider," shot ahead of them and then put his horse in a position that kept them from passing. There was a moment when Rosalind was certain that their horse would go crashing into the other one, but Sir Willton, also skilled as a whipster, pulled on the reins at the critical moment.

As Sir Willton fumbled for his pistol, Rosalind slid from the saddle. Her hastily devised plan was to divert his attention while Julian put himself in a position of advantage. But Julian had his own plan of action. He raised his crop once and brought it down on the other man's wrist, and the gun slid from Willton's hand.

"If you prefer firearms say so. My choice would be fisticuffs, so if you will dismount I shall do likewise. Unfortunately there can be no mill in the presence of a lady," Sir Julian pointed out. "However, we can meet at a later time and I shall teach you, fool, that it is not at all the thing to try to ruin the name of an innocent."

Sir Willton threw himself from his horse and Julian alit also, but in a more leisurely manner. The pistol lay on the ground between them, and it was Julian who moved more quickly and scooped it up.

"If you know what is best for you, Turncroft, you will count yourself lucky if you do not find a bullet in you. I am not in the mood for killing this morning, although I own that when I met the three on the road back there, my first impulse was to shoot you down like the dog you are. They explained everything to me," he said to Rosalind. "And a baser circumstance I have yet to come across. Come!" His voice grew a little softer. "You will ride with me until I can hire a rig at a posting house. I keep horses at such places on the way back. As for you," and he turned to Sir Willton again, "I wish not to look upon your face again for my leniency is beginning to run out."

Sir Willton, his face wearing a sullen frown and yet looking a little afraid, did as he was ordered. When the sound of his horse's hooves grew fainter and then died away completely, Rosalind turned and said in a failing voice, "Oh, how shall I ever thank you, Sir Julian? But for you . . . Do you know what he intended to do?"

"The very much incensed tutor was all too eager to tell me. He tried to insist upon coming with me but that would have left the other two to make the long journey on foot."

Although he gazed directly at her as he spoke, there was a distracted manner about him and he suddenly asked, "He is in love with you, is he not? Matthew, I mean? It was easy to see, from his anguished expression and the tone of his voice, that he is not indifferent to you. May I ask what your feelings are in that regard?"

Surprised, she could not answer him for a moment. Then, not quite steadily, she said, "It is the strangest thing for you to ask, sir. It cannot be the custom for a gentleman to ask a lady what is most deeply in her heart."

"True enough. But you see I have grown most exceedingly fond of you, my dear Rosalind. And," he added hastily, "your sister as well."

But not enough to give her a noticing glance now and then, she thought. What sort of game was he playing? she wondered. And how could it concern him in the least if she returned poor Matthew's regard?

"We will say no more on that head," she said coldly. "And let us waste no more time in starting home."

Sighing a little, he helped her up onto his horse. Of all the well-bred young ladies—and those who were slightly déclassé as well—who had come into his life and slipped out of it, he could not remember any one of them who had affected him as did this spirited girl whom nothing seemed to defeat. Her face was smudged with weariness as well as with grime. Her hands were dirty, and her hair was sadly mussed. There was exhaustion in her eyes and yet they remained cool and determined. In her bedraggled dress, its material too thin for the chilly morning, she looked more striking than if she had been a duchess in ermine and coronet.

He wanted to take her into his arms and remove from her shoulders all the burdens of someone who must care for a troublesome brat of a brother and the fade-away airs of a painfully shy sister.

He could not, of course. He did not want to frighten her and, being a man without conceit, he was sure that she saw him only as her cousin's suitor. As did most people within their circle of friends and acquaintances. And he knew that he must do something about that soon.

The journey back to the small outbuilding where Freddy and his friend had been held prisoners seemed shorter when it was taken in reverse. There was no reason for Sir Julian and Rosalind to enter it; but she pointed out to him that the shoe box containing the ten thousand pounds must still be where she had hidden it.

It was there, its paper wrapping damp from the morning dew, and when she lifted it out of its resting place, she handed it to Sir Julian soberly and said, "It belongs to you, I suppose. You were the one, were you not, who came forth with the money when it was needed?"

He did not want to think of the conditions of his supplying the money which, they had all thought at that time, was payment for the release of her brother. Actually, he did not want her to think of it, for she would naturally believe that the marriage settlement had been made in good faith and that his betrothal to Corinna had not been merely a matter of expediency. Whereas the truth of the matter was . . .

She interrupted his thoughts by saying, "Now that you have the package, shall we be on our way? I am sure you are much wearied, sir, for the day and night have been tiresome for you."

Her concern for him put him in a tender mood. He did not stop to think that there could not have been a worse place or a worse time to reveal what he was feeling.

"Rosalind," he blurted, "I must say this to you before

we overtake the others. I hold you in the highest regard.
Will you do me the honor of becoming my wife?"

Stunned, she looked up into his face, certain that she
had not heard him aright. Surely he had not offered her
his hand in marriage! The man whom she had promised
her sister would one day return that unwanted regard!
And who then, only the day before, had become betrothed to her cousin after months—years, actually!—of
courtship.

Was he funning? Would he burst out laughing in a moment or two and confess that it had been a joke to lighten
the monotony of the long ride?

Carefully she searched his face. There was no mocking
light in his fine deep eyes, only a glow which confused her
and made her turn away so that he would not see the
flush that burned in her cheeks.

She tried to remember what Aunt Mary had taught her
to say if she should receive an unwelcome offer. It had
fled from her mind, but after some thought, she was able
to utter the words.

"I am much honored, sir, that you should desire me to
become your wife. I regard you with the greatest respect
and were things different . . ."

"Gammon!" he cut in, angry with himself and not at all
with her. "Do not give me that polite answer. Rosalind,
my dear little love, what I have said is true; I simply said
it amiss. When we return home and you have had time to
think . . ."

Disappointed, wishing with all her heart that she might
accept this most obliging offer, knowing that she would
never feel for any other man what she felt for Sir Julian,
her eyes began to flash and she cried, "I do not know
your purpose in speaking of such a matter to me. You are
to marry Corinna. Then what sort of man are you that
you wish to become betrothed to two women at the same
time?"

"But Corinna . . ."

"I wish to hear no more, if you please." Fighting back
tears, her voice became sharper. "No doubt it amuses you

to play your little games. Well, you will never find my handkerchief thrown at you. And now if you—if you will kindly take me home!"

There was little said during the rest of the journey. At a posting house some miles beyond the scene of Freddy's imprisonment, Sir Julian obtained a fresh horse and a carriage somewhat worse for wear. It was, however, roomy enough to be comfortable even when they overtook the other three. Matthew's job horse was left behind for the time being, and even if Rosalind and Sir Julian had been in the mood for conversation, they would have had little chance to be heard for Matthew, his spirits restored, prosed on and on about the experiences Rosalind would have been happier to forget.

They were met at the door by Sir Charles and his lady. Hugs and kisses were exchanged; Jim was given a room over the stable; relief fading, Freddy was roundly scolded and promised punishment.

And Corinna, running downstairs and seeing Sir Julian in the hall, promptly burst into tears.

22

Corinna, her mama said, was becoming the veriest
wateringpot. But her tone was indulgent and she added,
most understandingly, that all young ladies were overset
and emotional when first they accepted a suitor's offer.

"As I was myself, you may believe. Bannestock will so
tell you. For many months he dangled after me and when
finally I consented to accept his hand, you would have
thought I was wearing the willow, so easily did I burst
into tears. However, once the vows were said and I became his wife, I was the happiest of women, for whatever
you may say about Bannestock, he has made me an unexceptional husband and I, if I may say so, a most complaisant wife, never trying to keep him the length of my
apron strings, although that is not exactly what I mean—
only that if he has interest otherwhere, I close my eyes as
a good wife should . . ."

Having entangled herself hopelessly and hearing Sir
Charles clearing his throat as a warning signal, she finished lamely, "Happy as I know you are, dear love, you
must turn a cheerful face to the gentleman who has done
you the honor of offering his hand to you."

She began then to babble about the notice of the betrothal being sent to the newspapers. "With everything
that has gone on here these two days past, I have had no
time or inclination to do so."

Rosalind saw that Sir Julian and Corinna were ex-
changing glances which seemed to be full of meaning. He
nodded, as though acknowledging what she was saying to
him silently. "Lady Mary," he said clearly enough to cut
over her lighter tone. "I wish we will allow the discussion
of betrothals and weddings to be postponed, for a short
time at least." He paid no heed to her gasp and the fluttering hand which she placed against her breast. "It is just
that—well, perhaps you did not notice when I spoke. I
told you about my brother whose regiment engaged with
one of Boney's. He has been these past four years in the
95th company and has suffered, I am led to believe, an
injury to his leg where a bullet entered it.

"You will forgive me, I hope, for speaking of this unpleasant subject in these circumstances, but it may be that
Foster will be coming home before long and I cannot
imagine my taking part in a wedding without him standing
at my side."

"Oh, yes, Foster to be sure." Her ladyship's voice was
edged with ice. "I should prefer that we not wait, but of
course your brother must be accommodated."

Another glance passed between Corinna and Wickstead. None of this did Rosalind understand. How could
Lady Mary speak so indifferently about a young man who
had been injured in battle during a tour of duty on the
peninsula? Not only indifference but even aversion was in
her manner; and if there was some reason why she had
taken him in dislike, for civility's sake at least, she could
have spoken less coldly about Sir Julian's brother.

"You have all had a most trying ordeal," she said,
changing the subject. "Rosalind, you may have Lizzie
bring to your bedroom several jugs of hot water and then,
having bathed, I am sure you will welcome the opportunity to lie upon your bed until you are well rested. Harriet, you will see to it that your sister is comfortable and

undisturbed. You, Corinna, will join me in the sewing chamber and we shall take up once more the subject of your bride clothes."

She cast a defiant look at Sir Julian and that, too, Rosalind failed to understand. What had happened, she wondered, to cause this drastic change in Lady Mary's mood? Was she so chagrined that the wedding would not take place immediately that she made her good-bye pronouncement to her daughter's future husband with bare civility?

It was days before her questions were answered.

The family was gathered once more in the yellow drawing room. There was one difference this time: Matthew Traynord was present at the conference.

"Because," said Sir Charles in his new, stern manner, "he has thrust himself into the situation and may be able to tell us something which pertains to it." He held up a hand quickly as Freddie's tutor opened his mouth to speak. "You will have your chance before too long, Traynord. Now, if you please, Freddy, we will listen to what you have to say. Please do not make speeches. We are not interested in your views on the downtrodden masses. Keep to the subject. A valuable piece of jewelry has disappeared. A servant none of us knew very well is also missing. You have persisted in claiming that she is not a thief. Explain, if you will, how you happen to have reached that conclusion."

"I have come to know her," his nephew returned stoutly. "We had many a good talk while she was here."

"A good talk with a servant?" Sir Charles's eyebrows rose to great heights. "How can that be? I fear, my young sir, that you have much to learn. There will be no more consorting with that class of people, do you understand me?"

Freddy muttered something rebellious under his breath but would not repeat it when requested to do so. There was a touch of defiance in Matthew's manner, too, when Sir Charles turned to him and accused, "If he had been properly trained and the right sort of ideas put into his head, we would not be in this unhappy situation. He would not have gone off on his wild goose chase, that wretched woman would not have been permitted to remain in this house in the first place, the rose pin would be in my hands at this moment."

He looked around at the others, each one in turn receiving his frowning glare. "You must all share the blame for its disappearance. You, my lady, for not keeping a firmer hand in the affairs of this household, you two," looking at his nieces, "because you have allowed your brother to have his head in all matters and were, I believe, the ones who brought that old woman into the house in the first place; and you, too, Corinna, for the pin belonged to you and you should have guarded it more carefully."

Unused to scolding from her father, Corinna immediately burst into tears. Lady Mary ran to comfort her, her round face indignant and her voice sputtering angrily. "You shall not ring a peal over this poor girl's head!" she cried. "She is not to blame at all. Oh, will the day never come when she will become Lady Wickstead and thus move into her rightful place and surroundings which will do her credit."

"And what," her husband asked pettishly, "is the matter with her place here?"

"The truth is out, is it not?" Lady Mary lifted her small nose. "The Bannestock fortune turned out to be not at all as it was thought to be. If that were to be known, think what would happen to our position!"

Freddy laughed jeeringly. "And you believe that matters? People may drop dead from hunger and exhaustion and yet the so-called high-born worry about their appearance of consequence! What sort of world. . . ?"

"I have had enough from you these past few days," his uncle warned. "Perhaps my mistake was letting you remain here instead of sending you away to school. Yes, perhaps I shall do that now. Since your tutor seems to have failed in what he should have done for you, why do we not consider the alternative?"

Rosalind, subdued and quiet until then, lifted her voice in protest. "You shall not send Freddy away. He has done nothing worse than try to help those less fortunate than he. At least he has a tender heart, does not turn his back on others . . ."

She broke off then, appalled by what she had said and the tone in which it had been said. Before she could apologize, Lady Mary put in, "Ungrateful girl! How dare you speak to your uncle so—he has always been too good, too kind to you? I do not know what has come over you young people suddenly."

"It is very easy to understand!"

They all turned, surprised, and looked at Harriet who had spoken. "It is that miserable little piece of jewelry which has set you all about. Since it has come into this house, there has been nothing but unhappiness."

She was flushed to the roots of her hair and Rosalind, at least, knew what great effort it took for her to speak in this uncharacteristic manner. But Harriet went on, saying what she evidently felt she must say, and the others listened. There was no other sound in the room except her voice. Low and gentle as it was, every word was firm.

"You are quarreling with each other, and that is something I have never heard between you until today. Love," and with the utterance of the word, her flush deepened, "seems to have been pushed aside and—yes—greed taken its place. You are all so concerned with a silly little pin that you have no thought for what has been suffered for it."

Rosalind stepped forward, but Sir Charles waved her back. "Let her go on," he ordered. "Miss Harriet seems to have something to say. It is seldom we have heard her express an opinion. Perhaps she feels that it is her turn."

Undaunted by the sarcasm of his tone, Harriet lifted her chin and swept a glance around at the others. "Do you not see what you are doing? Freddy went off to find the woman who has been accused of stealing Corinna's precious pin. He did a dishonest thing—oh, Freddy, my love, you know it is true! Then Corinna must become be-

trothed to Sir Julian so that there would be money
enough to pay for Freddy's return. And poor dear Rosalind—do you not all know what she suffered in this
whole miserable affair? How close she came to losing her
good name at the hands of that villainous Sir Willton? If
Julian—forgive me!—Sir Julian, had not rescued her, she
would be ruined."

A little sob rose in her throat. "She is the best of all sisters, yet who among you has given a thought to what she
has had to endure?"

"You must not believe that," Matthew spoke up in a
voice so loud that it seemed to echo from the corners of
the drawing room. "I, at least, have done all in my power
to protect her, would lay down my life if it would be
needed for her safety and happiness. Yes, you may stare
at me so but surely you must all have seen evidences of
my devotion. Alas, my feelings for her must remain un-
spoken for I have little to offer such a pearl above price.
Present circumstances, however . . ."

"Traynord, you are saying too much," Sir Charles said
wearily, "and there is no one here, I am persuaded, who
cares to listen to your prosing. As for you, Miss," and he
directed his stare to his niece, "I have found your tirade
most enlightening. Pray go on. I am sure you have more
to say."

But Harriet, as though realizing only then what she had
done, pressed a hand over her mouth, turned and ran
from the room.

23

It was a subdued household during the next few days.
There were few visitors. Corinna declared herself not in
the mood for social affairs and no invitations had come
for the other two young ladies. On two occasions Rosalind had heard Sir Julian's voice in the first-floor
drawing room and had quickly withdrawn to her bedroom, not wanting a face-to-face meeting with the man
who had offered for her hand in marriage. Still puzzled by
that strange circumstance, she spent much time in wondering what she should do: try to forget the matter or reveal to her cousin that the man she was planning to marry
had also proposed to her?

She came to realize that it would be impossible to follow the second course. For Corinna was not, these days,
her usual sweet-tempered, lighthearted self. She seemed to
be, in fact, moped and not at all in the mood of a young
lady who had captured London's most sought-after matrimonial prize.

At times Rosalind heard Lady Mary and Corinna deep
in talk as she passed the bedroom door of one or the
other. It did not sound as though they were discussing the

girl's bride clothes, for there was no joy in Corinna's voice, and that of her mother was sometimes sharp.

No announcement had yet been sent to the newspapers, and Rosalind knew that her aunt was irked by the future bride's refusal to allow the betrothal to be made public. But Corinna evidently was adamant, insisting upon waiting for the ceremony, as Sir Julian wished, until Foster Wickstead returned home from the peninsula.

After her outburst, Harriet became even more retiring than she had been before. She refused to speak of the day she had accused her aunt and uncle of being too concerned with a small, inanimate object—of being, in fact, greedy. She had suffered great embarrassment later, when she realized what she had said and done; but Sir Charles was not a man to hold a grudge and Lady Mary's favorite form of punishment was to remain silent while in the offender's presence, not realizing that the silence was more welcome than her steady stream of chatter.

Freddy, too, had grown quiet, but that was a circumstance which made his sisters uneasy. He was devoting himself so conscientiously to his studies they wondered what he was planning next.

His change in habit gave his tutor some free hours and he was spending many of them with Harriet. Sitting beside her while she was busy with her mending and embroidery, he would talk on and on with scarcely a pause for breath, and Rosalind amended her thinking from "poor Matthew" to "poor Harriet."

"What in the world does he find to talk about?" she asked her sister one afternoon when he had gone, at last, to the schoolroom. "He seems to have no difficulty in choosing subjects. For he proses on and on for, it appears, hour after hour. What," she repeated, "does he say to you?"

Harriet replied quietly, "Mostly it is about you."

Rosalind, wishing that she had not inquired, said, "Oh, nonsense! You know what Matthew is like. He wishes to make a drama of everything, and I refuse to believe that he is in earnest when he talks without putting periods to his sentences. But what," she asked, curiosity getting the better of her, "does he say about me?"

"That you are the kind of wife he has been looking for these many years. That he has formed a deep attachment for you. That he intends to offer for you when his appointment comes through. Dear sister," she asked with some anxiety, "are you sure you are not completely indifferent to Matthew?"

"As sure as I am of anything. We should not deal at all, for he is serious-minded and I am far from that. I get in the worst of scrapes and he would have no patience with that. I would not suit him at all, and you must discourage him, Harriet, when he talks in that vein. There is but one . . ."

She tightened her lips before the words slipped out concerning her real feelings. For only one man in the world had she a *tendre* and this one thing she must conceal even from Harriet. She did not blame her sister for listening with sympathy to the man's outpourings for she, too, knew the pangs of unreturned love. Still, she thought it wise to avoid spending time alone with Matthew and was determined to keep out of his company whenever possible.

She must develop a talent for evasion and stealth, she thought wryly, for now there were two of them to avoid: both Sir Julian and Matthew. In both cases, it proved impossible.

On a fair day, when she was returning home from the lending library, she found Matthew waiting on the front steps and realized, with a sinking heart, that he was waiting for her. He swept off his hat as she reached the steps and came bounding down to join her on the sidewalk.

"Fortune has favored me at last!" he cried. "How many times have I prayed that we might meet in just this way—alone and with nothing to divert your attention from what I needs must say to you. Come!" He took the books from her with one hand and held her elbow with the other. "We will walk along together, and I shall tell you what is in my heart."

"Matthew, please, I must go inside. Aunt Mary will be wondering where I am, worrying, perhaps, if I am away too long."

It had been the wrong thing to say and she realized that only when the words were spoken. Matthew immediately leaped upon them, twisted them about for his own purpose.

"Indeed she will not! It makes my blood boil to see you passed over and ignored, not given your real value. She cares not for anybody but that precious daughter of hers, who for some reason has developed fade-away airs."

"Matthew!" Rosalind protested. "You must not speak so of Miss Corinna. She is the dearest girl, unselfish and kind-hearted. Too, she is your employer's daughter and should this sort of talk be repeated to Sir Charles, it would be very bad for you indeed."

"I care nothing for that," he said recklessly. "For I shall be called to the school at any minute now. As soon as that happens, we will obtain the license . . ."

"Matthew," she said again, more loudly this time, "you are running on like a fiddlestick! I have no intention of marrying you now or later." Then, remembering the form of refusal in cases like this, she said, "I am much honored by your offer, Matthew, but I cannot accept it, obliging as it may be."

He stopped short, put his hand to his chest and dropped the books onto the sidewalk. He seemed stunned by her refusal. Taking his hand from her elbow, he curled his fingers into fists and struck one of them against his forehead.

"I have spoken at the wrong time!" he cried in great remorse. "I should have waited until I had more than my heart to offer. If you have no *tendre* for me now, it will come in time, perhaps even after we are married. It is not unknown that one party in a marriage may not be inflamed by love when first they are joined in matrimony.

Then with the living in close proximity, respect will lead to affection and affection to love."

"I wish you to listen to me," Rosalind said in a gritty voice. There were several passersby, a boy sweeping a cross walk, a delivery truck with a curious driver. "Matthew, you are providing much amusement for strangers with your heroics."

"I care not a fig for any of them!" he cried defiantly. "If you will only give me a favorable answer I shall be the happiest man in the world."

"That I shall never do." Her voice was so firm that she saw his expression change, become for the first time uncertain. "Matthew, it is not gentlemanly of you to refuse to take with grace a turn-down. Please believe me. No matter how many appointments you receive nor how much you urge me, I will not become your wife."

Believing her at last, he blinked his pain-filled eyes, and with his shoulders sagging, he turned and walked away leaving her to pick up the books scattered over the sidewalk.

Her encounter with Sir Julian was briefer by far and the pain was hers.

Haybolt, considering the gentleman almost one of the family, gave his grudging smile at the visitor and waved him toward the staircase. His eyebrows went soaring when Sir Julian revealed that he had come to call upon Miss Rosalind and wished to see her alone.

He was escorted into one of the smaller drawing rooms and Haybolt was pleased to discover the young lady playing idly on the pianoforte in the music room with no companion. How he would have explained this strange circumstance to his mistress he shuddered to think. But he returned and summoned Julian to the little room.

Rosalind turned about on the stool and saw with both trepidation and a singing in her heart the tall figure of her caller striding across the threshold. She half rose and then fell back. She could not think of any way to escape, for Sir Julian was blocking the door to the room.

He wasted neither time nor words. "My dear girl, why have you been avoiding me?"

She tried a denial, but lying always confused her and the lie was easily detected. She muttered something about being busy, but her voice dwindled away. Then she fell silent.

"Do not attempt to pull the wool over my eyes," he said gently. "You are like a ghost who disappears at the first sight of me. Rosalind, are you angry because of what I said to you outside that wretched shack near Sussex?"

"Not angry, no." It was scarcely more than a whisper. "At first I thought you were quizzing me. And it seemed to me a cruel thing to have done. But I cannot believe that you would act thus. I have never known you to hurt anyone for your own amusement."

He said dryly, "Thank you for that, at least. There have been times when I thought you considered me an ogre, so barely civil were you. My dear love, was it that you had a certain feeling for me and were repulsing it—and me?"

"You are a man of great conceit," she told him, making an effort to sound calm and reproving, "if you think, sir, that I had formed an attachment for you. No, it was—it was Harriet, and although perhaps I had better cut out my tongue before telling you, it is true that she has deeply admired you from afar for a long time."

There! She had told him the truth at last and the great lightness of relief made her giddy for a moment. Then, the dizziness passing, she said, "You will, I am persuaded, not let her know that you are aware of her feelings. I tell you this only so that you may understand her somewhat strange attitude toward you. I did hope that you two might," and her voice began to drift away, "make a match, but now I see how foolish were my dreams. You would not suit at all."

She was becoming appalled by what she had done. Not only had she tried to force her sister into a marriage never destined for her and in which she would have been excessively unhappy, but now she had revealed to this man the secret Harriet had so successfully hidden.

"But," she said wonderingly, realizing the truth for the first time, "I do not think she is wearing the willow. Whatever love she imagined she felt for you must have been the notion of a young and silly girl. Harriet," she mused, "has never known many young men. It is not to be wondered at that you dazzled her with your air of consequence, your fine features, your great civility. I do not think she really hoped you would pay her any notice. You were more to her like the hero in a romantic novel."

She searched his face, anxious that he should understand what she was trying to say. His smile was so tenderly amused that she dropped her eyes quickly.

"And you, my dear one? Have I dazzled you, too?"

"You must not speak to me in such terms." She tried to make her tone severe but did not succeed. "I am not your 'dear one' nor certainly, your 'dear love.' You are my cousin's future husband. I can never lose sight of that. I must ask that you, too, remember it. And there must be no more of these meetings alone."

He asked, "Then you do not care to trust me? If I tell you the truth will soon be revealed, you will not wait until then before you judge me?"

"I cannot." She turned her back and stared down at the keyboard of the pianoforte. When she heard no sounds of his leaving the room, she twisted her head about. He was still standing there, a rueful expression on his face, and she wanted to run into his arms; if she could have done so just this once, she thought she would ask for nothing more in her whole life.

"There is just one more thing I wish to say before you banish me forever." His voice was light for such a sober moment and when she turned slowly, she saw there was a twinkle in his eyes. "Are you not interested in what has become of Sir Willton Turncroft?"

He had been in her mind from time to time during the past few days. Sir Charles, upon learning of the near abduction to Gretna Green, had vowed to horsewhip the young nobleman; Matthew, with the least encouragement, would have sought out Sir Willton and presented his card, even Freddy, who claimed to despise the mores of the quality, offered to be his tutor's second.

Interested in spite of herself, Rosalind found herself crying truce. "I should like to hear, if you care to tell me. I expected never to see him again and have not done so. Has some misfortune fallen Sir Willton?"

"A most regrettable one, at least from his point of view. Two nights ago, very late, he was leaving White's and was followed down a dark street by someone who had been lying in wait for him. He was badly beaten to such an extent that his features seemed to have been rearranged. Unable to show himself in public in those circumstances, he has evidently repaired to his country seat and will remain there until his wounds heal and he can face his friends and acquaintances again."

"And the one who caused him such pain and grief, is it known who he may be?"

"No and never will be, I fear."

And upon those words, Sir Julian sketched a bow and quietly left the music room.

24

There was a short space of time when nothing event-
ful took place in the house in Grosvenor Square. Corinna
and her mother exchanged sharp words now and then, but
the quarrels were short-lived and trivial. Sir Charles, a
worried man these days, was absent much of the time, re-
plying, when questioned by his wife, that he was trying to
mend the family's fortunes and was having only a little
luck doing so. Matthew, when he and Rosalind met face
to face, wore an aggrieved air which she found embarrassing, and so she tried to avoid him as much as possible.

Harriet's championship of Freddy's tutor was con-
stantly surprising. "You have not let yourself learn to
know him, for you have been too busy trying to make a
match for me with Sir Julian. I hope you have given up
that idea, for I know now that I have not formed a real
attachment for him and that all I felt for him was no
more than a missish dream."

"But, my dearest sister, you deserve . . ."

"I deserve nothing except what I earn. Much as I dislike to ring a scold over you, I cannot help but say, as
dear Papa so often said, that there are times when you are

all about in your head and lead us all into scrapes. We
cannot remain here much longer; surely you see that? We
are an added burden to Uncle Charles now that his fortune has dwindled. I think, too, that they are not convinced that the disappearance of their precious pin is not,
in some way, our fault. Now if you were to marry Matthew, we could all still be together . . ."

"I shall never marry Matthew," Rosalind said stoutly,
"not for that reason or for any other. We shall wait a
while and if things do not take a better turn for Uncle
Charles, we must make other arrangements. You are right
on that head. You need not concern yourself, Harry. I am
able to take care of all three of us."

But her voice did not have the ring of confidence in it
which Harriet was used to hearing when her sister spoke
in that manner. Both of them fell silent, each with her
own plaguing worry.

Rosalind had not heard it for some time, that sound of
weeping in the dark hours of the night. Unable to sleep
herself, she was passing Corinna's bedroom door on her
way to the library downstairs to find a book and the sobbing came to her ears. Hesitating only a moment, she
scratched on the door and, receiving no answer, turned
the knob and went in.

A guttering candle burned on the bedside table and in
its light Rosalind could see little but enough to see that
Corinna's pretty, frilly chamber was untidy as she had
never seen it before. A gown was tossed over a chair, as
though thrown there when Corinna had removed it. One
silken slipper was near the door, its mate across the room.
A pelisse hung on the door of the closet, its edges trailing
upon the carpet; there were a reticule, handkerchief,
dance souvenirs, and invitations in a heap on the top of
the dressing table.

Corinna was huddled among her pillows, crying as
though her heart were broken. When Rosalind patted her
shoulder and asked in a soothing tone what the matter

was, Corinna turned with streaming eyes and cried, "Get out! Let me alone!"

"I wanted nothing more than to help." Recognizing the great pain which made her cousin lash out in that manner, Rosalind spoke gently. "I will leave if you so wish, but I fear you will make yourself ill if you go on like this. Can I not do anything for you?"

"No." Corinna turned her face back into the pillow and her voice became muffled. "There is nothing anyone can do. Mama . . . But why do I keep going over and over that? I made a promise and there is nothing for it than that I keep it. Please, please, I do not wish to talk of it anymore." Then abruptly she sat up and took Rosalind's hand. And she said the thing that was most puzzling of all. "Dear cousin, I am very sorry."

And for the rest of the night Rosalind lay sleepless trying to make sense of Corinna's words.

Few visitors had come to the Bannestock house during the days which followed the theft of the rose pin. Those who had arrived had been told firmly by Haybolt that her ladyship and the young ladies were not receiving. But one was more insistent than the others and refused to be turned away. Lucretia, Lady Fairlake, who claimed to be Lady Mary's closest bosom bow, could, in any fair contest, stare down the most formidable butler in the world.

"Something is going on which is being hidden from me," she told herself. "I know not what, but I have a feeling that it is so. Can it be that Sir Julian has, at last, offered for Corinna? No, that cannot be, for Mary would be only too eager to spread the news. Has that odious nephew of Sir Charles caused some trouble so grievous that they must hide behind locked doors? I am persuaded that is the answer and I shall not allow that it keep me from the side of my dearest friend."

She was a woman who lived upon gossip and the misfortunes of others. Her husband, who had many interests outside his home, provided her with no companionship, and caring nothing for intellectual pursuits, she had a

great deal of idle time on her hands. Her favorite topic of
conversation—outside the latest scandal—was her
mother-in-law, the dowager countess who, she claimed
with an air of martyrdom, would yet be the cause of her
death.

On the day that she faced Haybolt and threatened to
remain on the front stoop until she was admitted, she was
much agitated by a circumstance in her own life. Rushing
past the unhappy butler, she crossed the hall and hurried
up the staircase to where she was sure she would find her
friend. Breathless, for she was a plump, soft-fleshed
woman, she cried out at the sight of Lady Mary sitting
alone in her small drawing room.

"My dear, you must discharge that officious man!" she
gasped. "Will you believe that I had a most disconcerting
task of forcing him to admit me. As though I did not
know that you would want more than anything to have
me with you! Tell me, dear Mary, what has been going on
here? We have been as close as sisters since we were children, and I am ready to share your trouble, your sorrow.
What is it that keeps you hiding from the world?"

"I am not," Lady Mary said pettishly, "hiding from the
world. And you are most unobliging to tease me. No,
there is nothing at all that you must know."

It was plain that her friend did not believe her, but she
folded her lips tightly and refused to say another word on
that topic. "Dear Lucretia," she said with firmness, "let us
change the subject."

"Gladly. I shall take this opportunity, I most sincerely
hope, to be shown the famous rose pin which was handed
down by Bannestock's mama. It so happens that whenever
dear Corinna wore it, I was not present at that function.
Whenever Corinna and I meet, it is not on her person. I
think today will be a perfect time for you to show it to
me. I have heard so much of its beauty, and just think, in
but a few minutes I shall be feasting my eyes on it!"

The feast, Lady Mary informed her, must needs be
postponed. The only person to have a key to the box in
which it lay was her husband and he was gone from the

house, having left two days previously to visit his mother's country estate.

"So I must ask you to excuse me." She peered into the other woman's face, wondering if her lie had been accepted or if Lucretia could possibly have knowledge of the fact that the pin was missing. Possibly she had heard something from the servants; nothing could be kept secret when there were large staffs in the kitchens.

At that moment, Lady Fairlake began a discourse on her own servants. Each one, without fail, was lazy, slatternly and dishonest.

"Indeed I have my troubles," and she sighed deeply. "But none as severe as the suffering I must endure from Fairlake's mama. Such a tiresome old lady she is! Today I am more overset than usual about her, for she has played one of her worrisome tricks and thrown the whole family into a furor. She had been visiting her other son and his wife in Manchester. Then, after sending a message to us that she intended to extend her visit by several weeks, deceitful creature that she is, she did not return home and where she is God in heaven only knows. Visiting some of her rackety friends, I do not doubt."

She sighed and put a plump hand upon her breast and it moved up and down with each drawing of her breath. "Fairlake, worried that she has come to some tragic end, blames me for not, as he says, keeping a closer watch upon her. As though I were a nursemaid! Her age is five-and-sixty and she will soon, naturally, be at her last prayers. Must I follow her from place to place and restrain her from getting into scrapes?"

Lady Mary, growing bored with her friend's complaints and not at all interested in the disappearance of the Countess of Fairlake, sought diversion.

"I cannot imagine why Haybolt has not sent up tea when you are anxious, I do not doubt, to return home at the first possible moment, so worried you seem. Yes," she said with commendable guile, "you will be much more comfortable if you are there to welcome the poor, dear lady when she returns from what, I am sure, was a harmless little jaunt."

She went to the bell rope to summon Haybolt, and it seemed ages before he appeared. Her patience frayed by that time, she asked sharply, "Why has not tea been served as you know it must be when I am receiving guests?"

Haybolt offered both apologies and an explanation. "Two of the housemaids are sick with the toothache. Another is having her day off. The footmen are in the stables. I am left with only one servant and she is . . ."

He was about to say more but, his face wearing a most peculiar expression, he fell silent.

"What is it you seem afraid to tell me?" Lady Mary asked impatiently. "Come out with it, for we shall go without our tea completely if you stand there fidgeting all day."

There was a scratching at the door, and Haybolt went to answer it. A very small person in a shabby dress upon which was pinned an exquisite piece of jewelry, entered carrying a large tray.

She grinned at Lady Fairlake and said, "Never thought to find me here, did you, Lucy? But it stands to reason, because I like a lively place where there's a bit of fun now and then, not like the dull and deadly boredom of the Fairlake mausoleum."

Lady Fairlake did not hear the last few words; she had fainted dead away.

25

Sir Charles Bannestock arrived home unexpectedly early to find his household in a state of great confusion and excitement. His lady and the younger members of the family were in the smaller first-floor drawing room, as were Haybolt, Biggers and Freddy's tutor. Freddy was not present, scorning such things as ladies swooning for what seemed to be no good reason, smelling salts being waved about and babbling voices asking questions which no one answered.

The master of the house let his eyes fall upon the grinning little housemaid who seemed somehow familiar to him. It had been a long time since he was a young buck out on the town, but he could remember a certain much sought-after belle, some years older than he who had crowned her come-out with the greatest success, having married a most eligible *parti,* an earl to be exact.

There was no resemblance between the small, exquisite Isabel Clansbury and this gray-haired, wrinkled person who was in his drawing room for what reason he could not think. But he sensed some quality in her and he went across the room to where she was standing and said in what was, in the circumstances, a quiet voice: "Who are you and what are you doing here?" When she went on smiling, not answering, he turned to his wife and demanded, "Perhaps, Madam, you can explain this to me? How comes it about that your friend lies prone upon our sofa and this woman—a servant one would guess—wears upon her dress the Bannestock rose pin?"

It was as though he had not realized until that moment that it was so. His voice rose higher on the last word. His wife stared mutely at him because Lady Fairlake opened her eyes at that moment, lifted her head up a little way and cried, "It is Fairlake's mama!" and then sank back into unconsciousness again.

Lady Mary repeated, "Fairlake's mama!" and seemed about to faint also. But curiosity and affront kept replacing each other on her flushed, round face. She started to speak sharply and then, as though remembering to whom she was speaking, her voice fell into respect; but only for a moment, because the sight of the rose pin on the old lady's dress fired her anger again.

She had met Isabel, the Dowager Countess of Fairlake, no less than three times when she had been first introduced into society. But that had been a long time ago and she could not have been blamed for not recognizing the crone as Lucretia's formidable mother-in-law. Besides, whoever looked full into a servant's face and could be expected to know his or her identity if not clad in livery or uniform?

Sir Charles spared her the necessity of deciding in what manner of voice she should speak to the duchess.

"Perhaps you would care to explain to us, Madam, why you have upon your person the piece of jewelry which has been in this family for many years and which now belongs to my daughter. I hesitate to think . . . that is, I do not wish to . . ."

"Cry thief?" she put in, in an effort to be helpful. "No, you should not. For I have not stolen your silly little pin." She did not notice his painful wince, for she was struggling with the tiny gold bar which held the piece of jewelry in place. "I did not steal it, Sir Charles, but found it."

Three voices from different parts of the room echoed the words. "Found it!"

"Indeed that is the truth." Her eyes met Corinna's, and she said accusingly, "Carelessness, Miss, is the worst thief of all. Were you my daughter, I should punish you severely for not taking better care of something so valuable as this."

Sir Charles exclaimed indignantly and then, as though remembering her age and station, stopped short and growled, "Where did you come across it, my lady, if I may ask?"

"As indeed you are entitled." She bowed graciously. "It was a night when she had been escorted home by the man she is to marry—at least so you all seem to think, although I have my own opinion on that head. No doubt she had not seen to fastening the pin carefully enough and it is a wonder that it did not fall away in some other place while she was dancing. No real harm is done, and so I shall put it back in your hands."

She stretched out her own. As Corinna came forward slowly, the countess said, "Let it be a lesson to you, Miss! Although I do not think, knowing what I do about it, that this little gewgaw belongs rightfully to you. I knew your mama fairly well," she said turning to Sir Charles, "and I well recall her telling me that it has been handed down to girls bearing 'Rose' in their names. How does it happen then that I found it in the wrong one's possession?"

At that, Corinna burst into tears. Her mother, fastening upon the old lady a glare of anger, cried, "See what you have done! You might have returned the pin any time these past few days and spared us all worry and distress."

"Oh, do not speak to her in such a manner!" Corinna sobbed. "For she is right. The pin has never rightfully belonged to me and I have had no fondness for it at all, and I *wish* you will give it to Rosalind! I do not doubt that none of these dreadful things would have happened had she had it in the first place."

"You are overset, my love," Lady Mary said soothingly. "We will talk it over at some other time."

At that moment Lady Fairlake, evidently hearing the end of the conversation, sat up and cried, "But why cannot you speak out fully now? Mary, you have been keeping much from me and I am not sure I shall ever be able to forgive you!" She pushed aside the smelling salts bottle which Biggers was attempting to hold under her nose and twisted about to look at her mother-in-law. "You had best do some explaining, Madam, for Fairlake is sure to be much incensed—of that I am sure—when he hears the full story of what you have been up to."

"When the day comes," the countess said calmly, "that I am intimidated by my son, I shall be ready for the grave." She drew herself up and in spite of her smallness of stature, to say nothing of the shabby but clean clothing, she looked very much the noblewoman.

"I need offer no explanations to anyone, least of all you, Lucretia, for God in heaven knows that I am old enough and have been spared wits enough to do as I please. I believe that I have been cursed with the most boring family ever put upon this earth. Yes, my own son, Lucretia, and you seem to have caught the disease from him. What dull lives you live! Never a bit of fun, as I have said before. So I counted myself entitled to a little adventure, and I have always been curious about how working people live, and how the poor wretches with no money at all manage to survive. So I became Molly, which was the name of a nursemaid I was particularly fond of as a child. And these two obliging young ladies," she smiled at Harriet and Rosalind, "brought me into this house and befriended me. I hoped to learn many things and so I did, the most important that there are young people who have kind hearts; and I made a friend, dear Freddy, who cares about those less fortunate than himself."

As though the speaking of his name brought him into their presence, Freddy came rushing into the room crying, "What is going on here? It sounds like a nest of . . ."

He checked suddenly, his eyes found the small figure standing straight and firm and his voice drifted away.

Then, as though there were no one in the drawing room except the two of them, he ran to her side, crying, "Molly! Molly! You have come back!"

He went to her and because he was somewhat taller than she, he slid to his knees to take her into his arms. She pressed his head against her shoulder and murmured, "There! There! Everything is all right, dear boy. I am exceedingly sorry that I have caused you worry, but that is my only regret. Come, you must get to your feet for emotion is considered by some to be embarrassing and not quite the *ton*."

He got up slowly, bending his head so that it would not be seen that he was wiping away a tear with the back of his hand. "Do you think I care a fig for that? And if they think to accuse you of stealing that wretched little piece of jewelry they will find that I am on your side!" He glared fiercely at first his uncle and then his aunt. "Because you are of a lower station than themselves, they will try to take advantage of you. But I shall not permit it. I do not care about who you are or what you have done!"

His voice grew louder and stronger. "If they turn you over to the Bow Street Runners, I shall leave this house never to return . . ."

"But you have already done so," Sir Charles said wearily. "And it did not fare well for you. Let us have no more speeches, if you please. The countess will not, of course, be subjected to questioning from that quarter."

Freddy cried, "The countess! But who are you speaking of?" He looked down, bewildered, at the old lady at his side. "Something most strange is going on here, and I fear it is something I shall mislike when I learn the truth of the matter."

"It will be explained to you," Rosalind promised him, "when you are calmer."

Unexpectedly, Matthew spoke up. "I think Master Frederick has the right to know everything since it concerns him also. When one is kept in the dark, one imagines unspeakable things much worse than the facts themselves. We are, each of us, gifted by nature a brain and sensibility, thus we are higher than the animals. Frederick has a lively imagination and thus it is worse for him to be kept in the dark than were he someone who might be content to be sloughed off with half an explanation, something vague and not precisely the truth. In my opinion . . ."

Sir Charles, looking even more tired, interrupted him, too. "I do not think that any of us here are interested in your opinion, Traynord. We seem to have enough on our plate without your unending prosing. The whole thing opens my eyes to certain facts. I do not understand, however, how Freddy has been able to learn anything at all, for it appears that he and his tutor spend all their time prosing at each other."

Then, in a quiet, deadly voice, he discharged Matthew. "I shall give you a letter, and I doubt not that you can find another position. In a household of deaf mutes, perhaps, who will not have to listen to your never-ending speeches. I shall give you your salary until the end of the month and you may leave at any time."

Both Rosalind and Harriet cried out in protest. It was not the first time their brother's tutor had come close to dismissal, but on those other occasions, there had only been threats. Now it was to be seen that Sir Charles was adamant. Matthew seemed neither taken aback nor dismayed.

"Truth to tell," he said calmly, "I was waiting only for you to return to inform you that I shall be giving up this position. After some months of waiting, I have been informed that my application for the post of educationist at a boys' school in Manchester has been accepted. I shall leave as soon as it is convenient for you."

Freddy added his voice to his sister's cries that Matthew would be sorely missed. They pleaded with him to reconsider. "But," Harriet said a little sadly, "it will be better for you, I am sure. We shall miss you, will we not, Roz?"

"Immensely," her sister agreed, privately hoping that Matthew would not embark on one of his long dissertations, for once he got going he might reveal that he had offered for her hand in marriage; for he had been waiting only for this appointment, as she well knew, to once more press his suit.

He did not, however. He left the room walking tall and straight, looking not at all like a man who had just been discharged from his position.

Lady Fairlake, somewhat recovered from the vapors brought on by shock, hoisted herself up from the sofa and said with no note of enthusiasm in her voice, "Come, dear mama, and let us be on our way soon. You have worried sufficiently your son and the other members of the family because of your silly escapade. Lucky it was that you did not catch some despicable disease from the wretched people you met. No," and she held an imperious hand as the countess opened her mouth to speak. "I do not wish to talk of the matter now or at any time in the future. We must only hope that the story does not get around to our friends, for I could easily be ruined by the scandal."

The dowager countess sniffed. "Think of how much amusement you will be denying those silly, hen-witted women who think they are all the crack and have nothing to do except indulge in gossip."

She reached up and kissed Freddy on his flushed cheek. Then she turned to the three girls whose amazement still left traces on their expressions. "I wish you well, my dears," she said gently. "I am an old woman who has lived a long time. Let me give you a bit of advice: Listen to your heart and choose the right man. For married life is long, and if the choice is the wrong one, life can be a misery. Do not let anyone persuade you to accept the man with whom you are not in love."

All three lowered their eyes, each one convinced that what the woman had said was meant for her ears and hers alone.

26

Corinna came into Rosalind's bed chamber that evening and insisted upon bestowing the rose pin on her. "For it has caused trouble and unhappiness since Papa brought it into the house. Perhaps that is the reason; having been given to the wrong person, it might have developed an evil influence—like a curse."

Rosalind laughed lightly. "Dear cousin, you have been reading too many romantic novels. It is too beautiful to have anything of evil about it. Why do we not share it?" she asked as though in sudden thought. "When it goes well with something you are wearing, you must put it on. I, too, will do the same."

But she knew, even while she was speaking, that she would not do so. Her short interlude of being a sought-after newcomer on the London scene was over. Many men had professed to admire her. She had even had several offers, almost all of them from ineligible *partis*. Now she was suffering the fate of many young girls in their first season. At first they received more invitations than they could possibly accept; then, the novelty of their presence wore off and all that remained for them were the secondary diversions: the theater, the afternoon stroll, parties in the drawing rooms of people who were not quite in the swim.

Rosalind was reconciled to an unsuccessful season. She had never liked the idea of being on exhibition for any man who was hanging out for a wife. She and Harriet both, she was sure, would dwindle into old maids, but the prospect of that did not discompose her as much as the idea of marrying a man for whom she had no *tendre*.

When "Molly"—it was taking her a little while to remember that the woman who had worked in their kitchen was actually a member of the nobility—had advised the young ladies to "listen to your heart and choose the right man," she had been speaking the words of wisdom as Rosalind well knew, looking into her future. But the right man for her did not know his own heart. How could he do so when he had offered for one young lady while betrothed to another? The memory of that strange proposal plagued her, for she wondered where her duty lay and whether or not she should reveal to Corinna what Sir Julian had said on the morning when they had found Freddy.

There were other elements of strangeness which puzzled Rosalind and changed the atmosphere of Sir Charles's household.

What had suddenly happened, Rosalind wondered, between her and Harriet? They had always been the closest of sisters, friends as well as kin. Every secret had been shared, every innermost feeling revealed. And now, beginning almost with the day when Lady Fairlake had found her mother-in-law serving as the Bannestock's housemaid, nothing between the two girls was the same.

There were no more late-night confidences, discussions of what mild entertainment they might have attended, exchanges of opinions about the people they had met. Why that suddenly stopped Rosalind could not have said. Why Harriet insisted upon going immediately to sleep in the evenings was not to be understood. Rosalind was sure that sleep was not coming so quickly and easily for the girl who had become even more quiet and retiring than she had been before. When she had been suffering from unreturned love for Sir Julian, she had been, much of the time, flushed and nervous; now she had turned into a creature of moods, warm one hour, icy cold and silent the next.

"Dear sister," Rosalind pleaded when she could not stand the lack of closeness any longer, "can you not talk about what troubles you? You put me away when I would give anything I own to see you happy."

"It is all in your imagination." And Harriet turned away with a little laugh which became a sob. "There is nothing wrong, and I see no reason for you to keep teasing me about it."

"Is it Sir Julian?" Rosalind persisted. "Have you not, as you told me, recovered from your feeling for him?"

"It is not that at all," the other girl denied hastily. "I am not in the habit of lying," and she gazed straight into Rosalind's eyes in a truthful, direct manner.

During those troubled days, Rosalind looked back upon the time, early in her season, when the Bannestock house had been a happy place and wished that it might be so again. There had been Corinna with her angelic disposition, her sweet unselfishness, and a string of suitors dangling after her. The house had echoed with voices and laughter though sometimes there had been mild arguments, usually begun by Freddy and maintained by him until silenced by his uncle. Now it was not necessary to admonish him to be quiet. He spoke when spoken to, remained aloof to conversations between others, seemed preoccupied with his thoughts. And finally he informed his sisters that he would not be living with them much longer.

"For when I called upon the Dowager Countess of Fairlake today—how strange it seemed to be speaking her in that way!—she invited me to come to her on a visit. With Matthew leaving, it seemed a famous idea and so I told her. Then when she has found the right sort of school for me, she will take it upon herself to have me educated.

"For," he said with some of his old arrogance, "she considers me to have a remarkable brain and that I shall one day make you all proud to be my sisters."

Harriet and Rosalind could not but admit that Freddy had been offered a rare opportunity; under the sponsorship of the wealthy Lady Fairlake—eccentric as she might be—he would undoubtedly one day take his place in the world of men who made the laws and ruled the Empire.

Much as they dreaded the separation, they would not stand in the way of what would be, undoubtedly, a brilliant future. But there were a few tears shed upon his shirts that they were mending and the valise they were packing. And the gloom in the house increased.

Quarrels between Lady Mary and Corinna seemed to spring up at the slightest of excuses. And late one gloomy afternoon Rosalind, alone in the sewing chamber, heard a particularly lively one. It disturbed her that mother and daughter could speak to each other in such bitter tones, and she abandoned the clothes she had been making for Freddy and went to her bedroom to shut out the sound.

That evening Corinna did not come to dinner, which was a dismal, silent affair. Lady Mary left for a party; Sir Charles closed himself into his book room; Freddy, Matthew and Harriet engaged in a dispirited game of lottery tickets, which Rosalind refused to join when invited.

She was alone in her bedroom when Corinna scratched upon her door. Late as it was, she was wearing clothing for the outdoors, a dark cloak the hood of which hid her hair and shadowed her face. In one hand she carried a traveling case and in the other a reticule.

Her face was pale in the light of the candles in their sconces on the corridor wall. But her voice was firm when she said softly, "I am going away, dear cousin. I thought it best that one person in the house should know so that no one should be put about because of my going. I ask you only to keep from telling Mama and Papa until I am well distant. I can trust you not to let them know for at least an hour, can I not? You see, I must do this and before long you will understand . . ."

Rosalind spoke up sharply. "I shall never understand why you must needs worry your parents with some silly scrape. For it must be something of a stealthy nature that you would go off in such a manner. Come in!" She held the door open wider. "Let us talk about what you mean to do. You will feel better for it."

But Corinna refused the invitation. "I must not. Oh, Rosalind, I hope with all my heart that it is not another fruitless trip! You cannot imagine my disappointment when I went to meet Sir Willton at the Silver Crown. How cast down I was and have been ever since!"

"He is concerned in this?" Rosalind demanded. "How can it be so when it has been proved that he has a villain's black heart? Have you forgotten so soon how he tried to ruin me? Surely you are not going to meet him this night?"

"Do you think I have lost my wits? No, I have not laid eyes on him these many days. I merely said . . . No, Rosalind dear, I spoke of him only because . . . But there! I have no time to spare. Sometime you will know all. I ask you to do this one thing for me: When I have had a chance to get away, you may inform my parents of what I have said to you. Tell them, too, that I love them, but that there is someone whom I love more."

And then, with her hood over her face, she disappeared like a moving shadow. Rosalind stood motionless in the doorway. Her first impulse was to run downstairs in search of Lady Mary, who must have returned from her party, and Corinna's father who might still be at his figures.

Still undecided she started slowly down the staircase and then drew back at the sound of a man's voice in the first-floor hall. She could not distinguish anything of what he was saying but there was no doubt in her mind as to who was speaking. She would not at any time mistake Sir

Julian Wickstead's voice. It sent her back further, her hand clutched around the banister.

Within a few minutes they were gone. She heard the entrance door close softly and then, a few minutes later, the clopping of horses' hooves on the cobblestones.

She sank down on the staircase and covered her face with her hands. It was all too bewildering to understand. She could not figure out where they were going and why. They were betrothed, but not formally; there was no need for them to elope if that was what they were doing.

It would not have been like Corinna, at any rate, that genteelly bred girl whom even ambitious, matchmaking mamas admired for her pretty manners and unaffected ways.

Any time these past three years, Rosalind puzzled in her mind, Corinna might have accepted Sir Julian's hand. Why then this rackety drama of running off with him in the middle of the night?

She'd had, at least, some thought for her parents, sending a message to them, the delivery of which Rosalind dreaded. She continued to sit huddled on the stairs until she became chilled.

And then Harriet came looking for her and in whispered tones, Rosalind told her what had transpired and all that Corinna had said. Hand in hand, they went to awaken Sir Charles and his lady.

27

Rosalind had never seen her uncle in such a towering
rage. Testy as he had been lately, gruff and somber-man-
nered because of the reversal in his fortune, he had not,
at least, lost his temper in the presence of his ladies. On
that night when his daughter had walked from his house
with no word of good-bye, he paced the length of his bedchamber, his hair seeming to stand on end, and his face
so red and puffed with anger that it looked to be in danger of bursting.

His fine gray eyes burned with fury and while any other
gentleman garbed as he was might have lost his dignity,
Sir Charles's nightcap with a tassel dangling from its end
and his brocade dressing gown which left his legs bare
had no look of the ridiculous about them.

His anger was directed, first of all, at his wife. " . . .
For you drove her to it, Madam, and you need not try to
deny it. You knew her feelings for Julian Wickstead, as
fine a man as I have ever met and when I come across
him again I shall have a score to settle with him," he
shouted, unaware of the incongruity of what he had said.
"If he wanted to marry our lass, why did he take this

way? She is one-and-twenty and legally of an age to wed whomever she wishes. Tell me then, woman, why this foolish drama of running away in the middle of the night?"

In the circumstances her ladyship was holding up very well, had managed to find her own handkerchief and saturate it with cologne water and wave it under her nose. "It was a bargain," she said faintly, keeping then her eyes steadfastly upon her clasped hands. "Three years—that was what we had agreed. If by that time . . ."

"And when the date approached, you fell into a panic for you heard from one of your gossipy friends, no doubt, that you were not going to win that little game."

"Oh, Charles!" Her voice turned weak and quavery. "I did only what I thought was best. If it was wrong, I am sorry. I am not as clever, you see, as you are but it did seem to me . . ."

He growled, "Do not try to turn me up sweet, Madam. It will do no good." Then, abruptly, he turned to Rosalind and cried harshly, "You let her go without stopping her—how could you have done so? Evidently you have been in her confidence throughout this whole miserable affair."

Freddy and Matthew, hearing the commotion, had come to stand in the doorway, silent until that minute. Then Rosalind's brother cried out, "How unjust! Could she have stopped Corinna by physical force? I have not heard all the story, but enough of it to know that my cousin wanted to leave and she did. If she is ruined by some silly escapade, then it is upon her head and it will avail nothing for you to place the blame on anyone else.

"Each of us is responsible for our own actions." His voice grew louder as he warmed to his subject. "People like us at any rate. Some born to the so-called lower classes are victims of circumstance, born into poverty . . ."

"And that," Sir Charles interrupted, "will be enough from you. If you will stop making speeches long enough, you may consider that you, too, share part of the blame for this affair. Perhaps it was your going off in your little adventure that put the idea in her head."

"Rumgumtion!" Freddy said, not at all subdued by his uncle's glare. "Such a notion is beyond anything."

"Indeed I agree," Matthew put in. "It is natural, of course, when something oversetting occurs, to seek someone on whom to place the blame. It is difficult, you see, for us to accept our own guilt. So in this case, it is Frederick whom you are attempting to mount as the scapegoat. I do not pretend to know all the circumstances of this unfortunate situation. Whenever I saw them together—and this occurred not too frequently I must admit—it did not seem to me that Miss Corinna and Sir Julian had a true feeling for each other. Friendship, yes: that I will concede, and it cannot be denied that they shared a certain fondness for one another. Perhaps," and his forehead wrinkled as he earnestly sought for the right word with which to express his thoughts, "I would call it affection, the sort of feeling a brother . . ."

Only Harriet went on gazing at him with admiration after his speech was ended. The others appeared to have grown tired; there were surreptitious yawns. Even Sir Charles's voice had lost some of its fire when he said, "We have heard enough from you, sir. Enough, in fact, to do me for the rest of my life. As of this moment, you are no longer in my employ."

"But," Matthew pointed out reasonably, "you have already discharged me. I do not think it is necessary for you to do so again."

Sir Charles, defeated, mumbled, "I believe you are right."

The next day it was much like it had been when Freddy was missing. At every footfall heard from the street outside, someone would run to the window, pull back the draperies and peer out. Every sound of horses' hooves sent one of them on the same errand.

A story had been concocted for the benefit of the servants. Miss Corinna, they were informed, had been summoned to the bedside of her godmother who was at her last prayers. Since no one had ever before heard of this fictional old lady, it was doubtful if the story was believed by any member of the staff, but there was a grimness about the house that precluded their discussing it among themselves.

Only Biggers had received the confidence of her mistress, and that because Lady Mary had finally succumbed to her tattered nerves and needed the ministrations of her dresser. Haybolt, who had served the family long and faithfully for many years, had his own suspicions that there was something very much wrong, but would have allowed his tongue to be cut out before expressing them. Rosalind and Harriet exchanged few words that day, the elder sister seeming more cast down of the two and was found to have shredded into rags a perfectly good shirt belonging to Freddy which had needed only the turning of a collar.

There were no lessons that day in the schoolroom. Freddy wandered about the house like a lost soul; Matthew was busy sorting out his clothes and packing. Neither he nor Harriet appeared at luncheon, not as much of a coincidence as it might have seemed. For Rosalind heard their voices from behind the closed door of the music room as she passed it on her way upstairs. She was tempted to linger and eavesdrop but resisted, and the puzzlement about what they could be saying in such earnest tones remained with her all the afternoon.

There were conferences in the book room, with Sir Charles quizzing each one, about any little hint Corinna might have dropped or anything she might have said which had seemed insignificant at the time but would give some clue as to where she had gone and why.

The questions remained unanswered. With the strain of waiting, tempers flared, cutting remarks were said, and Rosalind wondered if there would ever be good feeling in the Bannestock household. When night fell and no word had been received from Corinna, every member of the family went to bed early. But if anyone slept, it was restlessly and Rosalind heard the prowling in the halls of those who gave up pretense of putting the cares of the day behind them.

Harriet remained in bed, sniffling now and then. The sound made her sister impatient beyond endurance. She wondered why Harriet was taking with so much grief the disappearance of her cousin, when she must know, as they all did, that Corinna had left of her own accord and evidently knew very well what she was doing.

She learned the answer the next day.

It was like a house of death, gloom hung heavy over everything. It was no time to be playing the pianoforte, but Rosalind sat picking out a tune on the keyboard for she had nothing else to do that would have engaged her mind.

Freddy came there to find her. Without preliminaries, he went directly to the subject that had brought him there. "And when, dear sister, do you mean to give Matthew his papers so that he and Harriet may be happy? You must know what you are doing to them."

She swung around to bring him into closer view. "I have no idea of what you mean. Matthew and Harriet? What can they have to do with each other? And with me?"

"I never believed you to be hen-witted," he said scornfully. "Can it be that you have not seen what' has been going on around here? They are in love, if that is what it's called. Have you not noticed that he has become the greatest moon-calf and she is the worst of watering pots? I cannot be persuaded that you have not seen how easily she cries. It is because she cannot accept the hand of the man she wants."

"But that is . . ." She had been about to speak Julian's name but stopped in time. Harriet had not been in love with the young baronet for a long space of time. But Matthew! She shook her head in disbelief.

"It cannot be. Surely I would have known if she were

feeling a *tendre* for Matthew? Oh, Freddy, you must be mistaken."

"There is no mistake. It only proves my theory that people do not see what is closest to them."

"But he was planning to offer for me. As soon as he got his appointment. How could he have changed so suddenly, and when he did, why did he not come and tell me?"

"You are a woman and so you do not understand things like this," Freddy said patronizingly. "No man who possesses the slightest knowledge of civility does an ungentlemanly thing like that. Suppose it was known by your friends and acquaintances, you would be the laughing stock of the city. Things like that are important to Lady Mary. Think how she would suffer if the news got out."

"What, then, should I do?" It was not only the fact that a romance had been blossoming under her very nose and that Matthew had transferred his affections so abruptly, it seemed not quite real that Freddy was taking charge of this tangle and handing out advice.

"Well, I have given the matter much thought. First of all, you must convince our sister that Matthew is not the man you want."

"As indeed he is not," she put in fervently.

"If you interrupt me, I shall get nowhere." His voice had grown severe. "Now, if people know that Matthew has thrown you over, it will be very bad for your credit. You are not a bad-looking girl," he conceded, "but there are many such on the matrimonial market. What I think is this: We will find a young man somewhere about and you will be seen with him frequently and it will be guessed that you have a new suitor . . ."

"No! No! No!" Her vehemence surprised him so that he stopped speaking in mid-sentence. "I am through with childish plots. I do not care a fig for what people will say! Who knows, at any rate, that Matthew considered himself—wrongly, of course—in love with me?"

She sat down suddenly and put her hands over her

eyes. "It is all such a wretched tangle. But there is something we can do." She looked up at Freddy and said with a constricted throat, "You will go upstairs and find them both. I have things to say to them."

They came with a look of apprehension on their faces, holding hands like a pair of naughty children expecting punishment. Harriet's eyes were dark with misery as she looked pleadingly at her sister. She seemed to be about to weep again when she blurted out, "Oh, my love, my best of all sisters, how can I tell you how sorry I am for all this."

Rosalind motioned to Freddy to leave the room. At the door he turned and said, "If you will take my advice . . ."

"I fear I will not do so," Rosalind said. "For I am not sure but things will grow worse instead of better." When the door had closed behind him, she studied the two uncomfortable young people. "First of all, I must tell you that I have never had any intention of marrying Matthew. If I did not make that clear, I am sorry. Never once did I entertain that notion."

Tears threatened to rise in a flood in Harriet's eyes. "You are saying that only because you wish not to distress us." She looked up at the man beside her and asked simply, "Who could not fall in love with Matthew?"

"I am glad that you have said that, dear Harry, for it is the way a woman should feel about her husband."

"H-husband!" Happiness began to peep out of the drenched eyes. "Do you mean. . . ?"

"That's exactly what I mean. You two must be married as soon as possible, so that you may go to his position as man and wife. This, I think, would be a very good time to announce your betrothal. In the circumstances, Lady Mary will not force upon you any sort of ball or party, which I am sure you would mislike. We shall begin immediately to get together your bride clothes."

A little shadow of anticipated loneliness slid over her heart but was soon gone. When she fell silent, Matthew, who had not been able to put a word into the conversation, now found his chance.

"I think, Rosalind—you do not object to my using your given name since we are to be brother and sister?—that I must give you an explanation . . ."

"None is needed," she said hastily, but he went on doggedly, while Harriet stared up at him as though each word were pure gold.

"You see, dear lady, you were like a bright, unattainable star in the heavens and I was a worshipper a million miles away. Never did I believe that you might accept my hand in marriage. You were merely there for me to adore. Many an ache I had in my heart," and he placed a hand over it and sighed, "until I found someone to give it surcease. Your dear sister with her sweet and gentle sympathy mended it and made of me a whole man again. I fear you cannot understand . . ."

"I do indeed," she said hastily. "And I believe you will deal exceedingly well. I am sure, Matthew, that you have many preparations to make before you take up your new position. And Harriet does also."

After a few more urgings, he consented to leave his beloved, his voice drifting back until distance silenced it. Rosalind crossed the room and put her arms around her sister. "Oh, dearest love, are you very sure? Can you be happy with him?"

"Ecstatically. Oh, Roz, I am the happiest girl in the world! When you talked of Sir Julian and my making an advantageous marriage, I longed for you not to plan such a future for me. And so you see," she said indulgently, "it was all for naught."

"But," Rosalind said, "the plan did work. There was a man who formed an attachment for me and then, when he saw I would not have him, turned to you for sympathy and found his true love. It was the scheme I concocted, except not the same man."

28

Another day and another night passed without any word from Corinna. Her mother took to her bed from time to time, but her periods of rest were of short duration, worried and overset as she was. Biggers fluttered about her with vinegar-soaked compresses and sleep-inducing potions, but Lady Mary would have none of them, preferring to bear her suffering with martyrdom.

When Harriet announced her betrothal to Matthew, what she considered another tragedy diverted her mind for a short time. She could think of a number of reasons why the marriage would be unsuitable. Freddy's tutor was not of their station; her niece was far above his touch. It would be thought among their friends and acquaintances that Lady Bannestock had failed to capture an eligible *parti* and she would be deeply humiliated.

Harriet, unsuccessfully trying to hide her radiant spirits in the face of the unhappy ones of the others, paid her no heed. In addition to the big fly in the ointment of her happiness—the disappearance of her cousin—there was a smaller one.

"My dear love," she said to her sister, "you will come

to live with us, of course. Perhaps not right away, for
Matthew insists that we have a proper honeymoon." She
blushed rosily. "But you must come to us after that, for
Freddy will be gone and I cannot bear to think of you
alone here. Corinna, of course, will be wed, and although
I doubt not that sometime soon you will meet someone to
whom you will not be indifferent, now I wish you to be
with us."

Rosalind, reluctant to put a damper on the other girl's
happiness, said, "Perhaps. Maybe later, when we have
you safely married." There was a false note to her voice
which escaped Harriet's notice. She began to murmur,
"Three dozen bed sheets at the very least. And pillow
slips to match. How lucky that we brought the linens
when we moved in here."

Lady Fairlake arrived that afternoon and Rosalind
whispered to her sister that it was almost magical the way
her ladyship could smell trouble, almost like an animal
with a faculty for running down a scent. Once again there
was an argument with Haybolt at the entrance door. Once
again Lady Fairlake defeated the poor man who strove to
follow her up the stairs into the small drawing room
where she was certain she would find her friend.

Puffing when he reached the threshold, Haybolt sought
to explain matters to his mistress. "I tried to tell her, my
ladyship. Well aware that you cared not to receive visitors, and so I told her. . . ."

Lady Mary lifted a hand which appeared to be
weighted with lead. "Some day her Lady Fairlake will call
upon us in the accepted way," she said with a touch of
sarcasm. "You will see to refreshments, Haybolt. Very
well, Lucretia," turning to the woman whose mouth and
chin trembled with agitation. "What is so important that
you have forced your way in? Have I not," Lady Mary
demanded of her friend, "enough on my plate as it lies
now?"

Then realizing that she was blurting out something she
would not have Lady Fairlake cognizant of, her little lips

tightened as though she did not intend to speak another word.

"Oh, you need not play the keep-secret with me!" Lady Fairlake bridled and then sat down opposite her friend. "I know all that has happened. Sir Julian's valet is courting my Betsy, my second housemaid you know, and when I coaxed her, she told me honestly what has happened."

She looked triumphantly from Harriet to Rosalind, who had been quietly listening to the exchange between the two women. "Perhaps, Mary dear, you do not wish the young ladies to hear what is being said."

Lady Mary, who looked to be on the point of fainting, murmured in a fading voice, "It does not matter. Soon the whole story will be known. I had hoped . . ." Her head drooped and Biggers, who had never been far from her lady's side during the past few days, rushed forward with her vial of smelling salts, but the hovering hand was pushed away with surprising vigor for one in such an agitated state.

"Coax!" she cried shakily. "If the truth be known, you no doubt threatened the poor woman with losing her place if she did not repeat the gossip to you."

"What a poor opinion you must have of me!" Lady Fairlake said, much incensed. "I have a mind to leave this minute and not tell you what I know." She half rose from her chair, but the temptation was too great and she sank back. "It should be that you know everything already. Surely you are in your daughter's confidence and although I am well aware that you have always misliked the match, I am persuaded that you can oppose it no longer. You see, the ship docked two days ago at Dover and that you should have considered, for I have watched her these three years and she has formed no attachment for anyone at all. A faithful heart," Lady Fairlake said with a sigh. "And now that she is one-and-twenty, she does not need your consent to marry the man she loves."

Rosalind felt as though her head was in a spin. She could make no sense out of the conversation between the two women.

"You made a bargain, did you not?" Lady Fairlake asked with a chiding note in her voice. "You told your daughter that you would consent if she would wait these three years. Now it is time for you to keep your word."

Lady Mary drew herself up with a militant gleam in her eyes. "I forbade it then, and I shall do so now."

Surprisingly, it was Biggers who spoke up on a firm authoritative tone. "You will not, my lady. You are a woman of breeding. Much as you may mislike what will happen, you will hide your feelings and pretend to the world that you are overjoyed that the young man has returned to these shores. You will make us all proud of you!"

"Well said!" Having completed her mission, Lady Fairlake arose and said, "I shall not wait for tea now. Later I shall return, for indeed I am most anxious to see the happy couple."

Corinna returned home three hours later. She was one of a small procession shortly after the family had arisen from the dinner table. All civilities forgotten, there was a scraping back of chairs and a rush to the entrance hall when the sound of her voice was heard.

Biggers and Haybolt were fluttering about, making the place even more crowded. Sir Julian was helping Corinna off with her cloak. There was a stout little woman wearing a cap that was somewhat askew who clutched at her shawl and looked about her with a mixture of curiosity and awe.

There was, too, a young man who appeared to be a few years younger than Sir Julian and while resembling him to some degree, would have done so more strongly if it had not been for the fact that his face wore a sickly pallor; he was thin almost to the point of emaciation, and his smile seemed to come with difficulty as though he were in pain. He leaned upon a cane as he waited for Corinna to return to his side, which she did the moment she was free of her cloak.

She took his arm and looked up at him adoringly.

Then, helping him across the hall, she led him to Lady
Mary and said, "Mama, here is Foster. It is wonderful to
have him back home!"

It was plain that her mother did not share her exulting
spirits. She looked with loathing upon the young man who
had returned from the Continent after fighting his country's war with Bonaparte. In that moment she knew that
she had lost her own war for Corinna, and she said softly,
"It was an age indeed that I waited for Foster, three long
years which it seemed would never end."

Lady Mary was heard to mutter, "Only a second son,
and nothing much in the way of a fortune."

But Sir Charles, exceedingly relieved that his daughter
was returned to him, closed the distance between them
and hugged her tightly. Then he put out his hand to Foster and said cordially, "Welcome into the family, my boy.
I was never in favor of the separation, things like that you
leave to the ladies. One of these days you must tell me
what went on over on the peninsula. As for you, sir," and
he turned to Sir Julian with a scowl which he meant to be
formidable but was not quite that. "I think you must explain why you took my daughter off in that manner at the
cost of her good name . . ."

"Indeed you are deserving of an explanation," the
young baronet said. "But as you must have guessed by
now, my future sister-in-law was too eager to see the returning hero to wait here. When it became known that the
ship was docking at Dover, she requested me to accompany her there, and so I did. But it was all most respectable, I may assure you, and Mistress Potkind will so
support me in that."

He turned to the plump little countrywoman and led
her forward so that she was standing in the center of the
group. For an instant she looked too shy and overawed to
speak, and then, catching Corinna's eye and receiving an
encouraging smile, she straightened her cap and said,
"Milord is right. Respectable it was, to be sure. For they
stayed at our tavern—the Blue Goose it is—on the way to
Dover, which I have no doubt was where they were going

since why should there be a lie about it? And then on the
way back they was to stop overnight—this time with this
poor young man, back from the wars as he was."

There were a few puzzled glances exchanged. Lady
Mary made the mistake of asking impatiently, "Why has
she been brought here if I may inquire? A tavern-keeper's
wife, I have no doubt. What has she to do with my
daughter?"

Mistress Potkind's eyes flashed sudden fire. "I am here,
milady, because the young gentleman would have it so.
And do not think that I am here for my own pleasure.
There is much to be done at the inn and Potkind needs
my help badly. Generous as milord has been in paying for
my services, there will be a long, tiresome ride in a post
chaise and he will be fretting—Potkind, that is. So do not
believe that it is a favor on your part to have me over
your threshold . . ."

"No, no," Corinna said soothingly. "Do not get into a
pucker, please! We are much in your debt. You see," and
she turned to her mother, "Julian felt as did Papa, that
my name might suffer, as though it mattered to me! He
has brought this good lady to assure you that there could
not be any cause for harmful gossip. For it was she herself who provided us with a chaperone when we were
forced to remain there both on the way to Dover, for I
was much fagged from the long journey. And coming
back, we saw only too plainly that Foster needed to rest."

The tavern owner's wife folded her hands at her waist.
"The young lady," she said primly, "occupied my best
front bedroom on both nights. Mine was beside it, and
being the light sleeper I am, I should have heard any
moving around. But there was none for fearing just such a
suspicion there might be, he insisted that I lock him into
the room where he spent the night—at the other side of
the house it is. On the night when they were returning
home, his brother occupied his bedroom, too, and it was
the same again. And so I am willing to tell the whole
world. The young lady was as safe as though she slept in
her own bed!"

The young lady she was speaking about was blushing rosy red. To Rosalind it seemed that Corinna had returned to her old self. Her face was radiant with a smile as she went to the sturdy little woman and hugged her. "You shall partake of refreshments with us and then the coachman will drive you to meet the post chaise. Do not hurry away, dear lady, for you have come a long distance this day to do us a favor. Haybolt!" and although she spoke to the butler, Corinna looked directly into her mother's face and said, "We shall all be served tea in the yellow drawing room after one of the maids brings hot water upstairs so that Mistress Potkind may refresh herself."

"And we have more to talk about," Sir Julian said in a determined voice. "And while we are all weary from the events of these past few days, perhaps making plans and explaining a few things will revive us. And it is best to have things settled as soon as possible."

It was he who did most of the talking after Mistress Potkind had left, and it had been made certain that Major Foster Wickstead had been made comfortable. The entire family was there: Lady Mary trying to arrange her features to look cordial, Sir Charles leaning forward to hear every word, Harriet and Matthew sitting close together on a divan, Freddy looking detached and uninterested. Rosalind, alone on the other side of the room, felt a little pang at the sight of the two couples so obviously happy in each other's company. She felt more entirely alone than she had ever done in her life.

With her eyes upon Sir Julian's face, she was watching the liveliness which played over it and had missed a few of the words he had spoken. It was hearing Willton Turncroft's name which caught her attention and sharpened her ears.

" . . . the worst of knaves. It was that piece of jewelry, of course. He wanted it so badly he did not hesitate to lie and cheat."

"It was my fault, too," Corinna confessed. "But I had

not heard from Foster for such a time. Word had reached me that he was injured and my head was filled with worry. When that odious man promised me that he knew how bad the wounds were and would tell me, and how it would be possible to get in touch with Foster, well, I think I must have been all about in my head to have believed him and gone to meet him at the Silver Crown."

She slid her hand into that of the man beside her. His other hand tightened over the head of his cane. Pale and drawn as his face was, it looked somewhat fierce as his mouth hardened and his eyes flashed.

"As soon as I have regained my good health I shall have something to say to Will Turncroft. I have known him since we were children, and he seems not to have changed. He always was a despicable worm."

"I believe," Sir Julian said modestly, "I have taken care of that adequately. At least I did my best."

"As you have taken care of all my concerns," his brother said affectionately. "You promised to do so when I left with my regiment and you kept that promise as I knew you would do." His hand tightened around Corinna's. "By seeming to court my girl you discouraged those who would dangle after her. When I was able to receive her letters, and yours, it was most comforting to know that you were protecting my interests. I knew, too, that you were doing your best to keep her from being too lonely. I have one more favor to ask you, good brother. I want you, of course, to be at my side when we are married. Which will be at the first possible moment. We have waited long enough for our happy life to begin."

Lady Mary opened her mouth but before she could speak, Sir Charles said uncomfortably, "There is the money from the marriage settlement. I hesitate to talk of such matters at this point, but it must be returned to you, Julian, since things have taken a different turn."

Sir Julian waved a careless hand. "It is all in the family. I have had some luck in the exchange with money Foster left with me. We will settle that among ourselves, and what you have now will serve as his portion. You are

right—we should not be discussing the subject now.
Rather, let us celebrate. If you will have Haybolt bring up
some champagne, sir, we can toast the happy couple. Or,
perhaps I should say, the two happy couples." And he
smiled at Harriet and Matthew, boldly holding hands but
wearing matching flushes when all eyes were turned upon
them. "It will be a race, I doubt not, to see which pair of
you reaches the altar first."

The champagne drunk, the toasts repeated several
times, Lady Mary sniffling at first and then growing more
amiable when she learned that Foster was not, after all, a
penniless soldier, the party broke up.

Rosalind could hear Corinna in a sweet and soothing
voice saying, as she led her mother upstairs, "You will
learn to love him and, after all, I did keep my promise to
you. Perhaps you were right. At eighteen, I might not
have known my own heart. If I had no doubts for the
whole three years . . ."

Her head down, Rosalind followed the sound of their
voices as they started up the staircase. But she had not
reached the first step when she found her way blocked.
Looking up she saw Sir Julian standing in her path. A
sudden flood of tears blinded her and to her horror a sob
came up in her throat. She turned away but his hand
lifted her chin.

"Why are you so unhappy, my love? What troubles
you?"

She sought wildly in her mind for an answer. "It is just
that I shall miss them all: Freddy, who will go away to
visit the countess. And Harriet who is to marry Matthew.
And Corinna, too, of course. Oh, Julian, I shall be so
alone!"

"Never," he said. "For you shall marry me. Did you
not know that that is what I have been hoping for these
many days?"

Now, her tears quickly dried, she could see his face
which was no longer shattered and swimming in her tears.
It was so tender and bright with love that her own be-

came radiant and she murmured on a note of great joy, "Oh, Julian, I do believe at last that you mean it."

"I shall spend all our years together proving to you that is so," and he drew her into the circle of his embrace.

Before she surrendered completely, she felt impelled to say, "But I have been such a silly widgeon. I have tried to arrange things for others and came close to ruining things for them . . ."

"You are exactly what I want and need," he told her, and he began indeed to prove it to her with a long, earnest kiss that left her breathless and the strong arms which held her close.

James A. Michener

Winner of the Pulitzer Prize
in Fiction

The Bridge at Andau	23863-6	$1.95
Caravans	23959-4	$2.25
Centennial	23494-0	$2.95
Chesapeake	24163-7	$3.95
The Drifters	23862-8	$2.75
The Fires of Spring	23860-1	$1.95
Hawaii	23761-3	$2.95
Iberia	23804-0	$2.95
Kent State: What Happened and Why	23869-5	$2.50
Rascals in Paradise	24022-3	$2.50
Return to Paradise	23831-8	$2.25
Sayonara	23857-1	$1.95
The Source	23859-8	$2.95
Sports in America	24063-0	$2.50
Tales of the South Pacific	23852-0	$2.25

8007

Buy them at your local bookstore or use this handy coupon for ordering.

This offer expires 1/7/81